"Kiss Me
Murmured

"Please, just this once. Kiss me . . ." Driven by
some dark force she could neither understand nor
control, she'd pulled his head down to hers and
captured his lips.

"Raine, my God, do you know what you're doing?
Do you know what you're asking?" The unfamiliar
feel of him only heightened her own wild
excitement. He tightened his hold on her waist.
"Listen to me. I'll say this just once, and then I
won't say it again. Stay away from me. Because if
you don't"—even in the shadowy night she could
see the dark, primitive glitter in his eyes—"I might
throw away the last scrap of integrity I have . . . and
take what you're so willing to give."

SHIRLEY LARSON

(also known as Shirley Hart) read her first romance in
1976. Two years and thousands of romance novels
later, she decided to try writing one. Her third novel
was accepted for publication, and she's been writing
ever since, loving every minute she spends spinning
romantic fantasies for herself and others to enjoy.

Dear Reader:

SILHOUETTE DESIRE is an exciting new line of contemporary romances from Silhouette Books. During the past year, many Silhouette readers have written in telling us what other types of stories they'd like to read from Silhouette, and we've kept these comments and suggestions in mind in developing SILHOUETTE DESIRE.

DESIREs feature all of the elements you like to see in a romance, plus a more sensual, provocative story. So if you want to experience all the excitement, passion and joy of falling in love, then SILHOUETTE DESIRE is for you.

Karen Solem
Editor-in-Chief
Silhouette Books

SHIRLEY LARSON
To Touch The Fire

Silhouette Desire

Published by Silhouette Books New York

America's Publisher of Contemporary Romance

SILHOUETTE BOOKS, a Division of Simon & Schuster, Inc.
1230 Avenue of the Americas, New York, N.Y. 10020

ISBN: 0-671-49999-8

First Silhouette Books printing April, 1984

10 9 8 7 6 5 4 3 2 1

America's Publisher of Contemporary Romance

Printed in the U.S.A.

BC91

To Susan and Georgia . . . with love.

Thanks go to the printers who answered endless
questions: Charles Edwards of Edwards Press in
Rochester, N.Y.; Larry and Norma Jean Ellis of
Cornerstone Printing; Arvis Hair, former Linotype
operator for the *Ayrshire Chronicle;* and Bob
Marcum, Linotype operator and printer for the
Appeal Tribune in Silverton, Oregon.

1

Raine Taylor braced herself against the force of the May wind blowing free and strong across the South Dakota prairie and pushed open the door of the school building. Her waist-length hair, its caramel sheen glowing in the sun, whipped around her face. Both hair and face were reflected in the glass portion of the door, but it wasn't her reflection that caught her attention. It was her hands, splayed out at eye level against the dark door-frame. Raine frowned. Her nails were clipped short and she had spent a good five minutes scrubbing them, but the dark shadow of printer's ink still made a tiny black half-moon under the tips of her fingernails. That's how printer's ink gets into your blood. Direct transference.

As if they had been painted on the glass in front of her, her sister's hands flashed into her mind. This morning, Michele's well-groomed fingers had gripped Raine's arm in pleading, and the nails, long and sleek with plum polish, had gleamed like out-of-place jewels against the beige of Raine's ink-spattered smock.

Michele. During the day, working at the print shop and fighting with the ancient Linotype machine, she'd managed to keep her worries at bay. But now, as she climbed the steps, those worries built into a tidal wave of tension that centered in the pit of her stomach. What was she going to say to Jade?

Muttering to herself that she was an idiot, she reached the top of the stairs and turned right. With any luck at all, the kindergarten class would be five minutes into their show and she wouldn't have to say anything.

She stood in the doorway and scanned the room anxiously. Sure enough, the play had begun. Tate, his curly hair ruffled around smooth cheeks pink with excitement, was standing holding a giant black letter L painted on an eight by fourteen cardboard. When Raine walked in the door, he beamed with pride. His eyes searched the space behind her, the hope in them tearing her heart out. But when he saw that his mother wasn't with her, his face fell. At that moment, more than anything else in the world, Raine wanted to wring her sister's neck.

The black-eyed cherub holding the E had just started to speak. Tate had assured Raine a hundred times that he knew exactly when to say his poem because they were doing them in alpha'bat'ical order.

Well aware that she was earning curious glances from everyone, both because her sister wasn't with her and because she hadn't yet seated herself, Raine dragged her eyes away from Tate. At the back of the room, those empty chairs waited—next to Jade.

It was all there, the lazy grace, the tall lean maleness, the hard profile. He was the only man in the room but it didn't seem to bother him at all. He sat stretched out on the chair looking supremely at ease . . . and supremely male. In a room filled with wall-to-wall wriggling children, doting adults and the overpowering aroma of glue, he still had the power to shake her to the low heels of her shoes. The old, familiar warmth tumbled through her bloodstream . . . only to be followed by the old, familiar self-hatred. *Fool. Idiot.*

"Hello, Mrs. Mitchell," she whispered to the dark cherub's grandmother who also wrote the local news items for Julia's paper. "Yes, I know I'm late. I'm terribly sorry. You know how busy we are on Friday. May I—please? Excuse me." She squeezed past Mrs. Mitchell's well-padded knees.

Jade's eyes matched his name and they shot a look of pure, unholy rage at her. Even before she'd crossed in front of Betty Brightwood, her knees began to shake and she was glad to sit down.

Her relief was short-lived. Jade reached over and grabbed her wrist. Startled, her eyes locked with his. He muttered darkly, "Where is she?"

"I don't know," she whispered back. That was the truth—as far as it went. Patty Harson, a slender intense woman with fire-engine red hair seated in the row ahead of them, turned around, and put her fingers to her lips.

"K is for Kettle so shiny and bright . . ." Kevin Harson grinned a wide grin, crossed his feet at the ankles . . . and sat down on the floor with a plop that was undoubtedly intended to shake the entire state of South Dakota.

She waited in stomach-wrenching suspense for her nephew to say the one line she'd been practicing with him for weeks. Tate's voice was soft, but he spoke clearly and well. "L is for Lantern that shines in the night."

Tate sat down, and Raine started to breathe again. Even at five, he had the lithe compactness, the easy sense of the boundaries of his body that Jade had. The Kincaid men were born with it, she decided. Tate already rode well. It was something her sister and Jade had argued bitterly about.

With a stinging awareness of every move he made, she felt Jade's head turn, felt him gaze at her. Determined not to betray how much he disturbed her, she kept her eyes focused on the front of the room, but she was so overpoweringly conscious of Jade watching her that she didn't have the vaguest idea what was happening. She was barely conscious of the children working their way through the rest of the alphabet and then jumping into a large iron kettle and crying in unison, "We've said all our names in one fell swoop and now we've become

. . . alphabet soup," but uppermost in her mind was the scent of Jade's clean skin, and the way he was looking at her. What was he seeing? Was he blaming her for his wife's absence? Oh, why couldn't Michele have come back in time?

Then it was over. Mrs. Dugan, a young, enthusiastic woman who wasn't much taller than her neophyte students, announced that punch and cookies would be served as soon as she and the children got the refreshments organized.

Tate strolled up to his father. "Are you staying, Daddy?"

Jade spread his jeaned legs and caught his son between his knees. His head tipped and his whole attention focused on Tate, Jade was infinitely more appealing than any man had a right to be. "I don't know. Are you sure the food is okay?"

Tate gave him the most scornful look he could manage. "You know it is, Dad. I helped make it."

"That's right," Jade said, heaving a theatrical sigh of relief. "You did. I just forgot there for a minute."

"Did I do okay, Aunt Raine?"

"You did fine, honey," she said, reaching out and ruffling his hair. It smelled fresh and clean; she'd helped him shampoo it that morning. Afterwards, she'd combed it for almost fifteen minutes until he was satisfied with the way it looked.

Now, looking up at her quizzically, he asked the question she'd been dreading. "Where's Mommy?"

"She . . . something came up and she had to go into Canton. She'll be back in time to fix your supper."

"I wanted her to see me in our alpha'bat' soup."

"I know. I . . . I'm sorry. She was sorry to miss it."

"Don't lie to him," Jade said in a low, lethal tone.

Appalled, she shook her head. "I'm not lying. She *was* sorry."

"She went to the tryouts then," Jade said in that same, brutally cold voice.

10

Raine could only nod. That was the end of the conversation.

Raine dared to look at him, pleading with her eyes for understanding. He only stared back at her with that lean, impassive face. Then Tate grabbed his hand and tugged him over toward the long table where the punch bowl sat. Raine thought she could use some, too. Her throat was very dry.

When the refreshments had been consumed and the event was over, she walked out of the room, Jade and Tate behind her. Jade said nothing as they trooped down the stairs but when they were outside, he said to Tate, "Go see if Lady is all right."

Lady, Jade's chestnut mare, was tethered to the bicycle rack. Unquestioningly, Tate trotted to the end of the sidewalk and tipped his head to look up at the horse. At his approach, the mare bobbed her head and whickered.

"You rode in," Raine said nervously, desperately grasping at conversation to stave off the attack. It didn't work.

"She came to the print shop before she left and told you she was going, didn't she?"

Raine thought of a thousand things she might say but none of them came out. "Yes." In the warm Dakota sun, she felt the heat of the afternoon beating down on her head. But that other heat, the one inside her, was far more potent. If Jade had been any other man she would have reached out and touched his arm. She didn't. She was always very careful never to touch Jade. Half laughing, Raine said cautiously, "She probably won't get the part anyway and you're worrying about nothing."

"She'll get it," Jade growled.

"She does have talent," Raine admitted. "She used to spend hours pretending she was someone else . . ."

"She still does."

At that, Raine ducked her head and hid behind the curtain of hair that fell on each side of her face. Her thoughts were far too dangerous to risk letting Jade catch a glimpse of them. When she had herself under control, she lifted her head. But there was no longer any need to hide. Jade was gone, striding away from her toward Tate, his back straight and unyielding . . . an indication of the anger he was holding inside.

He bent and untied the reins. She walked down the sidewalk to say goodbye to Tate, unable to take her eyes off Jade. She'd seen him unhitch a horse and climb into the saddle a million times. Why was it particularly stirring today?

Seated on the horse, Jade leaned far over to give Tate his hand. He pulled the boy up into the saddle in front of him and encircled Tate's waist with one arm. Tate soberly eyed her from his privileged perch. She looked up at them, the incredibly attractive man possessively holding the boy with his features and her sister's dark eyes, and told herself that her sister was a fool. She had the world . . . and she was tossing it away.

"Did she happen to say what time she might be home?"

Raine met his eyes, knowing how much male pride it had cost Jade to ask that question, knowing how much he would worry for Michele's physical safety until she was home. Even in the summertime, the South Dakota prairie was no place to be at night with a malfunctioning car or a flat tire. "No. I would have told you if—"

He cut her off. "Thank your aunt for coming to see you, Tate," he said, and the boy did as he was told.

Raine listened, her heart aching. With a slight movement of his wrist, Jade guided the chestnut around in a circle. She watched him ride away, his broad back shielding Tate from her completely.

Julia was still at the print shop when she got back. As Raine opened the door, the bell on it tinkled and banged, and Julia looked up, the half-glasses she wore for reading perched on her nose, her white hair slightly ruffled. At sixty-two, Julia was a warm, attractive woman. She had taken Michele and Raine into her home ten years before when the girls' parents were killed in an automobile accident. Julia had done everything humanly possible to ease the pain and loneliness for the two heartsick teenage girls, and Raine loved her dearly.

"You didn't have to come back. I've got the proofreading almost done. How was the program?"

"Very nice." Raine hesitated, schooled herself to sound normal. "Tate was the best one there, of course."

Julia's smile deepened. "Of course. Can you write up a few lines for the paper without revealing your blatant bias?"

Raine smiled. "I could try." Could she? She wasn't sure she remembered anything of what went on.

The shop was quiet, and Raine wandered around restlessly. Finally she went and got the push broom to clean up the slivers of lead that were scattered around the Linotype, like iron filings around a magnet.

Julia finished reading and put her arms back and stretched. "Did Michele say whether or not they can come to your birthday party?"

"I . . . she wasn't there."

Julia's arms dropped. "She wasn't there?"

"She went over to Canton to try out for that community play they've been advertising."

"Yes, we ran the ad, didn't we? *Mary, Mary,* isn't that the one they're doing?"

Raine nodded. "Michele's been practicing the part of Tiffany."

"Tiffany?"

"That's the name of a character in the play. She's sort of the . . . other woman, writes with brown ink, and dots her i's with circles." Julia raised her eyebrows. Raine quickly said, "That's a line in the play."

"How does Jade feel about all this?"

Raine made a rueful face. "Do you have to ask? I mean, this may be the age of women's liberation, but Jade hasn't gotten the word."

"Maybe it's just as well. It's part of his appeal."

"What is?"

"His refusal to reorder his life to conform to the rest of the world. Although," Julia cocked her head to one side, "I don't suppose it's the rest of the world Jade cares about. He only cares about Michele."

"Then wouldn't you think he'd listen to her?" Raine asked fervently—too fervently she realized as Julia stared at her quizzically.

"I think he has. But there's no real way they can compromise. She doesn't want to live here. He does. He's a true cowboy, tied to the land. And he's smart enough to realize it. Sooner or later . . ." Julia shrugged. "I tried so hard to talk to that girl before they got married. I knew she wasn't ready to settle down." Julia hesitated. "But I wasn't her mother and . . . that made it difficult."

It wouldn't have made any difference if she had been. Michele was wildly eager to marry Jade and had insisted on a huge, splashy wedding paid for out of her inheritance from their parents, a wedding that the good people of Verylon were still talking about. "Had to drive all the way over to Yankton and then when we got there, there wasn't a place to park. Too many cars, too many people." To the natives of the small town where Raine lived, ten people were a crowd. But Michele adored having people around her. The first year Michele and Jade were married, Raine spent more time out on the ranch than she did at school, until the day Jade told his wife that she was interfering with Raine's education. It was then, during that first year, when Raine was an impressionable sixteen-year-old, that she began to feel the pull of Jade's attraction. But shortly after she had discovered her wildly impossible admiration for him, she was instructed to stay away.

Being away from Jade was a welcome reprieve. She got involved in schoolwork and she dated Jade's brother, Marc. Then the year Raine was seventeen, Michele became pregnant. This time, Michele's pleas to Raine were insistent . . . and then tearful. Michele wouldn't be cut off from humanity altogether. She needed Raine. Couldn't Raine please come out to the ranch and stay for a few weeks? In the end, it was Jade's request that Raine come out to keep her sister company that brought her to the ranch.

When she arrived with her suitcase, Jade had carried it up to the spare room, his lips clamped together, his back straight. He said nothing, but Raine was painfully aware of his cool reception.

In the days that followed, she watched as Jade tried to placate his unhappy wife. Raine saw how gentle he was with her, how patient, how long-suffering. He wanted the baby, that was obvious. But Michele was inconsolable. She hated being on the ranch, and she hated being pregnant. She became petulant, and Raine spent hours riding around the ranch, using the excuse that she needed the exercise, when in reality what she needed was to give her ears a rest. She suspected Jade of employing similar tactics to save his peace of mind. Since Raine was in the house, he spent more and more nights on the range, nights Raine was quite certain he could have spent at home.

Later, around ten o'clock that night, after Julia and Raine had returned to the house and Julia had gone to bed, the doorbell rang.

Raine answered it, knowing it could only be her sister.

Michele stepped into the narrow living room with its embroidered doilies and old-fashioned furniture and somehow managed to make the very air in the drab little room crackle. Unlike Raine, Michele was dark-haired and vibrant and walked with a energetic gracefulness. "I got the part." Michele's dark blue eyes glittered and her voice was husky with the strain of the tryout and her excitement.

"Congratulations. When do rehearsals start?"

"In a few weeks." She sat down in the chair next to the sofa and let her eyes wander over Raine. "How did it go this afternoon?"

"Tate did beautifully."

"Not Tate," she said, waving her hand impatiently in a stagey gesture that dismissed her own son. "What did Jade say?"

Disappointment in Michele made Raine's voice sharp. She met Michele's blue eyes with a spark in her own gray ones. "He knew where you were. And he knew you had told me."

"Absolutely clairvoyant, isn't he?"

"He knows you," Raine said shortly.

Michele's eyes narrowed on Raine. Raine had showered when she came home, then she had changed into jeans and a T-shirt, and pulled her hair back with a leather and wooden barrette. She had left her face bare of makeup. She knew exactly what she looked like. At twenty-three, she'd long ago given up competing with her beautiful sister.

"He doesn't know me at all," Michele said slowly.

Raine stared at her. She had the distinct feeling it was a stage line, delivered for effect. "What's that supposed to mean?"

"It's cryptic," Michele said, smiling at her suddenly. "Isn't that one of the things that's so deadly boring about this prairie town? Everybody knows everything about everybody else. No one has any secrets."

"If you knew about them, they wouldn't be secrets," Raine said dryly.

Michele ignored her. "That's what we learned from Tony, our director, tonight. He told us that every character has a secret."

"What's Tiffany's secret?" Raine mocked. "She really doesn't use brown ink, she uses green?"

Michele gave her a scornful look. "Tiffany's secret is that she needs a man who sees beyond her beautiful body and loves her for herself."

"That's an original idea."

"Go ahead. Make fun of something you don't understand. That's typical small-town thinking." She stared at Raine. "I won't be like that. I just won't."

Raine rubbed a hand over her jeans. "Jade's probably worried about you."

Michele's lips moved in a mocking smile. "Is that a polite invitation to go home?"

"No," Raine said softly. "You know as well as I do that Jade worries."

"Ah, yes," Michele said, watching her with eyes like a tigress', "we both know Jade worries. The difference is," her voice went very soft, "I don't care what he thinks . . . and you do."

Raine averted her eyes, fastening them on Michele and Jade's wedding picture. "You did once. What happened?"

"I got bored. Married life is boring. I'm going out of my mind. If I had known what it was really going to be like . . ."

Raine looked at her. "You knew what life was like on a ranch."

"Did I?" Michele shrugged her shoulders. "I'd always lived in town with Julia and you." She studied Raine, a peculiar look in her eye. "You're the lucky one. You're free. You could walk away from this town tomorrow. I can't understand why you stay here."

Raine shrugged. "Where would I go?"

"Anywhere where people are," Michele said passionately, "a city where there are nightclubs and you can walk into a restaurant and order coq au vin or duck à l'orange."

"Have Jade take you on a trip," Raine suggested impulsively. "He can afford it. Have him take you to San Francisco or New York City."

Michele flared angrily, "I don't want a trip. I don't want to go and see what I'm missing and then have to come home to this . . . this provincial backwater." In her distress and excitement, she pushed herself up out of the chair, twisted and walked toward the door. "If I ever get a chance to get out of here, I—"

Raine, alarmed, made a sound of distress and jumped up. To her sister's back, she cried, "Michele, listen to me. You . . . can't leave. You have too much to throw it all away. . . ."

Michele turned suddenly and faced Raine. A mere nose length away, Raine could see in Michele's eyes a dark, primitive emotion. "But suppose I throw it in your direction? You'd like that, wouldn't you?"

Shock immobilized her. "I wouldn't—"

"Oh, yes, you would, sister mine." Michele's eyes glittered. "Why do you think I've stayed on this godforsaken prairie for six years? Because I knew, *I knew* if I left, you'd fall into Jade's arms like a plump peach, all ripe and ready to squeeze."

The shock dissolved into anger. "That's not true! You have no right to say that to me. . . ."

Michele laughed and whirled around. She exited on that line, perfectly timing her escape while Raine grappled with the nausea that threatened to climb her throat and the cold, self-hatred that gripped her.

Grimly, Raine went up the stairs to her room, thinking that the talent for acting must have been given to only one member in the Taylor family. How long had Michele known? Right from the beginning? She had spent hours with Michele, but they had never been close, not really. They seemed to disagree about so many things. They had only one thing in common—Jade.

She saw Michele only once during the next few weeks.

Her sister came into the print shop with a promotional article about the play and chatted with Julia as if nothing had happened. She was civil to Raine, and Raine tried to match her sophistication, but her stomach churned. She was relieved when Michele, with an airy goodbye, walked out of the shop.

Two weeks later, during the last week of July, when everyone was suffering from a heat wave that seemed to have no end, she lay in her bed in her short nightie and, for the first time in her life, thought seriously about leaving Verylon. Was she a fool to stay? What future was there in loving her sister's husband? Perhaps if she got out, got away, she would forget him. The perspiration collected on her back. Her room, on the west side of the house, had been like an oven since Monday. If it weren't so hot, maybe she could think, could decide. A cold shower might help. Would it disturb Julia? She threw back the light sheet and was on her feet when she heard the soft ring of the kitchen phone. She padded down the stairs in her bare feet, hoping to stop that ringing before Julia heard it.

"Tate's sick," Jade said in her ear, and even hearing his voice on the phone made her blood race in her veins. "I don't know what to do. I've called the doctor, but all I get is that confounded answering service and he hasn't called back."

"Does he have a temperature?"

"I don't know."

Raine made an exasperated sound. She'd seen Jade sit up all night with a newborn foal or a weak calf and stay as calm as a glassy sea, but whenever anything happened to Tate, he went into a tailspin. "There's an oral thermometer in the upstairs medicine cabinet. Have you been giving him aspirin?"

"No. I'll start giving him some right away. . . ."

"No, don't. Just give him a cool sponge bath."

"How do I do that?"

Worry about Tate and her own leaping nerves made

her say sharply, "For heaven's sake, Jade. Just pretend he's a sick calf."

"If he was a sick calf," the words were chilly, "I'd douse him with disinfectant and put him in with his mother."

Raine recoiled from the hard, cynical words. It wasn't the first time she had felt the backlash of Jade's anger toward Michele. And even though she wasn't her sister's keeper, she felt inexplicably guilty.

"Take his temperature and call me back," she told him coolly, fighting to keep the conflicting emotions that seethed in her under control.

He hung up, and she walked to the stove to fill the kettle. As she put it on the burner, the phone rang again.

"This thermometer doesn't work. It says his temperature is below normal."

She sighed. "You didn't leave it in his mouth long enough. It's hard to get the correct temperature of a young child with an oral thermometer. Get him to hold it under his tongue for at least three minutes and preferably five."

There was a silence. Then, through gritted teeth, "There's no answer at the number Michele gave me. When she stayed with you last weekend, did she say anything about her rehearsal schedule?"

Stayed with you last weekend. Shocked dumb, she tried frantically to make sense out of Jade's words. When she did understand them, a hard knot formed in the base of her throat and she couldn't force a word past it. The silence hummed over the telephone lines.

"No. No, she didn't," she said at last, the words too quick and anxious. "She didn't mention a thing to me." Truth surrounded by the largest lie of all.

The answering silence made her wonder if she had really fooled him. His voice sounded normal when he said, "I'd better go see if I can get a correct reading on that damn thing."

"If he only has a temp of one hundred to a hundred

and two, give him a cool sponge bath. If it's above that . . ." her voice faltered, "you'd better take him to the hospital. He could go into convulsions."

He thanked her and the click in her ear told her he had hung up the phone before she could take the receiver away from her ear.

The tea kettle began to bubble and she snatched it off the stove before its strident whistle woke Julia. She sat drinking her cup of tea, wishing she had told Jade to call her back. When another hour went by, she could stand it no longer.

The phone rang several times before Jade answered, and when he did, his voice was even more husky than usual.

She asked, "Did I wake you?"

"I was just dozing."

"How is he?"

"Good. The sponge bath took his temperature down and he's sleeping here in the bed with me."

She closed her eyes to shut out the mental pictures. "I'm glad. I was imagining him in the hospital."

Jade said nothing for a moment. When she opened her mouth to tell him goodnight and hang up, he said in a soft voice, "I should have called you back. I forgot that you would worry. I owe you an apology."

The deep, quiet warmth in his sleep-thickened voice warmed her from the ear next to the receiver down to the toes that were trying their best to curl into the kitchen floor. "That's all right. I know you were too worried about him to think of anything else."

Quickly, before he could reply, she replaced the phone.

When she called again the next day, Tate's fever had broken—and Michele had come home.

A week later, on Friday, the bell on the door of the print shop tinkled and banged. "Hello, Benjamin Franklin. How's the almanac business?"

She looked up and saw Jade's brother standing just inside the door. He was a tanned, slim young man with a shock of wheat-colored hair and a wide grin on his face. "Hello, Marc. Just getting by from day to day."

He groaned, twisted a chair around in front of her desk and straddled it backwards. "How are you and the monster getting along these days?" he asked jerking his head back at the Linotype machine.

"Okay. A few of the mats stick, but other than that—"

"Mats?"

"Matrices. The brass molds that make the lead slugs of letters."

He wrinkled his nose at the smell of the hot lead that still lingered in the air. "When are you going to convert to phototype and offset press like the rest of the world?"

"When our rich uncle bequeaths us eighteen thousand dollars to buy a phototypesetter and another eight thousand for a camera, not to mention an equally generous amount for a new press. . . ."

Marc held up his hand. "I get the picture."

She plucked at the collar of her smock. After the discovery that her sister had lied to Jade about her whereabouts, she had avoided him. Now she was even self-conscious with Marc. Marc smiled at her and appeared not to notice.

"Big brother has offered to take us to see his wife, the star, in the play tomorrow night and then out to dinner afterwards just like they do in the big city. Sounds like fun, huh?"

The last thing in the world she wanted to do was spend an evening with the two Kincaid men. "I . . ." She couldn't even say she was planning on going with Julia. Julia had gone the night before, and said that Michele was very good.

Across from her, his fingers wrapped around the top of the chair, Marc went very still. "You've been putting me off for two weeks, Raine. If you don't want to see me—" that Kincaid pride flying, "just say so, okay?"

"It isn't that I don't want to see you, Marc. It's that . . . well, things haven't been very good between Jade and Michele since she started this play and—"

"I know that. But tomorrow night's the last performance, and they'll be kissing and making up before you know it."

Would they? "Shouldn't they be left alone, then?"

He squinted at her and grinned. "For Pete's sake. They're married. They can do that when they get home." He rose and angled the chair back toward the wall. "Speaking of which, when are we going to get married?"

She met his comic leer with cool silver-gray eyes. "Well, not this afternoon. I have to proof three galleys." She bent her head and began to read, hoping he would take the hint and leave.

The soft voice that reached her ears hardly sounded like him. "One of these days I'm going to say that—and ask you for an honest answer, Raine."

She looked up at him, her gray eyes faintly mocking. "If I said yes, you'd be scared to death."

"Try me," he shot back.

In this mood he was infinitely appealing. "Not today," she said lightly. "I just told you, I've got too much to do."

"Tomorrow, then."

"For dinner, or marriage?" she teased.

"Take your pick," Marc said lightly.

She made a wry face. "If I have to choose, I'll certainly choose to eat."

Marc shook his head in mock sadness. "No romance in your soul at all, is there?"

"Actually," her tone was dryly amused, "eating is sensual."

"Explain," Marc said, focusing his light green eyes on her.

"Having to do with the senses." She kept her voice carefully light. "Three of them, actually: taste, smell and touch."

"I can think of something else that involves those three senses," Marc said, slowly unfolding his body from the chair.

She'd started this; she wasn't quite sure why. Now, with Marc taking the two steps toward her, she wished she hadn't. She regretted the impulse that had made her goad him. But she couldn't back out now. "What were you thinking of?"

She turned her chair slightly, facing him. He grabbed her wrist and pulled her to her feet. "Making love," he whispered into her ear. Unresistingly, praying she would feel something, anything, she stood in his arms. He brushed his mouth over her cheek and then kissed her, his lips warm and practiced. He held her gently, supporting her. He did everything right . . . and it was all wrong. He had kissed her before many times, but this time he demanded more from her, probing with his tongue. His lips seemed foreign, like something outside her existence. Marc was kissing her, and she had never felt so alone and lonely. In an effort to stave off the emptiness, she lifted her arms and circled his neck, drawing him closer.

The bell on the print shop door banged its warning and the sound echoed through her ears. She pulled away from Marc's embrace and looked across the desk—directly into Jade's hard face.

There was a sudden silence, as if a movie reel had stopped. Then Jade turned to Marc. "I saw your car outside." His voice was cool and matter-of-fact. "I just thought I'd stop in and see if you had decided to go with me tomorrow night."

Marc slid his arm around Raine's waist and pulled her around to stand next to him, facing Jade. "We were just talking about it."

"So I . . . saw," Jade murmured dryly.

Raine fought to keep her body from tensing. He smiled an indulgent smile that lifted the corners of that attractive, cynical mouth. "What did the lady decide?"

"She didn't really give me an answer." Marc turned to

her. "How about it, Raine? Want to go? Big brother's paying the bill, remember."

She met Jade's eyes and saw something there, a flare of emotion, but what it was, she wasn't sure. It was a betrayal of his feelings, though, and as if Jade were aware that something had gotten past his carefully composed face, he shuttered his eyes with amber gold lashes.

Did he want her along, or did he hate the idea of her going with them? She couldn't begin to guess. She only knew she wanted to be with him. "I . . . yes, thank you. I'd like to go."

This time, there was no mistaking the mockery in Jade's smile.

2

In the darkened auditorium, she sat between Jade and Marc. They were hardly into the first act when Marc grasped her hand and pulled it over into his lap. She felt the warm strength of his thigh, and wished desperately that it was touching him that made her heart beat faster. But it wasn't. It was sitting next to Jade, being so aware of him that she could almost feel the movement of his breathing under the soft caramel-colored suede jacket and the white silk shirt that he wore. Against Jade's trousered leg, the ruffles of her peach-colored sundress lay like bright swatches of light. It was incredibly intimate to sit next to him and listen to the soft sound of his breathing, to hear him chuckle as the inept hero sank deeper and deeper into trouble.

Then Michele made her entrance, and his breathing pattern altered. Raine could feel his nerves tighten as if they were an extension of her own. She hardly recognized Michele, and it wasn't just because her sister was made up for the stage. Michele *was* Tiffany; she moved and talked like a woman accustomed to a wealthy, luxurious life. Even Raine was aware that the audience loved her, and that Michele almost stole the show. She had—what did they call it?—presence.

When the play was over and the lights in the auditorium came on, Jade said, "The cast is driving over to Okoboji in Iowa. We're meeting Michele at the Outrigger. It's a restaurant and bar on the lake."

Marc's protest was immediate. "My God. That's eighty miles away."

"To theatrical people the night is young," Jade said dryly.

"Most of them," Marc argued, "have to get up and go to work in the morning just like we do."

"The leads and the director are from New York City," Raine said.

Jade gazed at her. "Yes." How could he say so much with that one tiny word?

They went out and got into the car. The long trip seemed endless. Her nerves alive with tension, Raine sat in the front between the two men and knew that this was the last time she would ever willingly spend an entire evening with Jade. His continuing presence tore her apart. His closeness made erotic fantasies spin through her brain like cobwebby threads of bright light. She saw herself touching his hands, playing with the fine gold hairs that grew from the backs, turning his palm over and pressing a kiss into it. She saw herself tracing the hard outline of his face, the square contour of his jaw, the lean line of his cheeks, discovering the prickly roughness. Michele complained about his beard constantly, wondering aloud how a man who was so fair could have such a rough nighttime skin. Raine had lain awake nights afterwards, her mind alive with vivid mental pictures . . . pictures of Jade, gloriously male and naked in a softly lit bedroom, inviting her to touch him, and finally, touching her. . . . Self-consciously, she ran her hands down over her skirt, gathering it toward her body and away from Jade's.

They drove through Spencer, one of the larger towns in Iowa and one of the few that was growing, and began the trek up through the tiny towns clustered along the highway. Jade slowed down and she looked out the window, watching as an amusement park came into view. The neon lights of the merry-go-round, the Tilt-a-Whirl and the roller coaster cast a watery rainbow on the surface of the lake. One Sunday afternoon, she'd gone with Jade and Michele to the park and after they had ridden all the rides, they'd collapsed on a quiet grassy knoll away from the carnival atmosphere. Jade, stretched out beside his wife, had moved closer to shade her body from the sun. He'd lain there, propped on his elbow, staring down at his wife for a long breathless moment while Raine's heart seemed to stop beating. Then he had smiled down into Michele's face . . . and kissed her. Her heart burning with an ache that was beginning to be a constant companion, Raine had looked away. That gentle, possessive smile haunted her dreams for years afterward. Would any man ever smile at her with that same combination of love, tenderness and protection?

She forced her mind away from the past and gazed out the car window. She hadn't been to the Iowa Great Lakes in years and she could see that there had been some changes. A landmark house next to the highway, a rambling, two-story affair with gingerbread trim, had been painted pink and spotlighted from the lawn.

They drove past the park, and Jade guided the car around a curve. Their destination was the restaurant on the street of shops created inside the old Central ballroom. She had never been there. Did modern people shop more than they danced? Maybe that was what was wrong with the world.

When they walked down the long hall that led past the stores, Raine smelled a delicious mixture of chocolate candy, cinnamon stick spice and cedar wood. The shops were all closed, of course, but their huge glass windows were lit from inside, displaying craft items. At the end of the hall, Jade pulled on the rope handle of a big wooden door. A sign that said The Outrigger bumped against the door.

Inside, it was cool and dark and nautical. The floors were rough and wooden. A mainmast wrapped with gray rope rose to a three-story ceiling and the wood walls were covered with more rope, old anchors and heavy chains. She wasn't sure if she'd stepped into a restaurant or onto the deck of a white slaver.

"What would you like to drink?" Jade's voice came from just behind her ear.

"Something . . . cool. A . . . Tom Collins, I guess."

"I'll have a Manhattan, brother," Marc told him.

The cast wasn't there. There were just a few people at the bar and two couples seated at tables at the other end of the room. Marc's hand at her waist guided Raine toward a table that commanded a view. Huge, floor-to-ceiling windows looked out over the lake. At least, she thought it was the lake. In the night, boats seemed to float over a dark, silvery surface that was so still it could have been land.

Marc held out a chair for her and, when she was settled, slid in next to her. There were two empty chairs across the table. Marc stared down into the little hurricane lamp that held a green candle. The flame burned erratically in the drafty open space of the room. "Pretty fancy place, huh?"

"It's nice," she agreed.

"What did you think of your sister? Wasn't she great?"

"She was . . . very good."

"Did you think so?" The soft question came from Jade, appearing beside them, bending lithely over to set their drinks on the table. Relieved of his burden, he sat down across from Marc, his eyes on Raine.

"Yes, I thought so." Desperately, she cast around for some other topic of conversation. "Oh, look, there are stairs and a deck down below where you can watch the boats out on the lake."

"How old is Michele?" Marc asked, sticking to the topic

that she most wanted to avoid. "She's older than you, isn't she? I know she isn't quite as ancient as brother here."

"She's twenty-six," Raine said reluctantly.

"Too bad." Marc shook his head. "I thought she was younger. She's really too old to be starting a career as an actress now."

Raine glanced quickly at Jade's face. Dazed, she said, "I don't think there's any question about her . . . starting a career."

Marc's shoulders moved lazily. "She's been bitten by the stage bug." He smiled at Jade. "Brother here may find himself commuting to New York on weekends."

Marc gazed at Jade, knowing full well he had thrown out a line of bait. Jade didn't take it. Instead, he looked at Raine.

"I forgot to tell you. Tate sends his love."

Raine felt her cheeks go warm. "I'm glad he got over his flu."

"You haven't sent me your bill." Jade's voice sounded amused and a smile played over his well-shaped lips.

Marc's curiosity was instantly aroused. "Bill? Why should she send you a bill?"

"I called her for a midnight consultation."

"I never did tell you how to give him that sponge bath."

"I figured it out," Jade replied.

A noise at the other end of the room saved them from having to explain any more to Marc. The door burst open and the cast, noisy and high with excitement, poured into the room. There were several people in the group whom Raine didn't recognize. She decided they must have been behind the scenes, doing props and makeup. The last few people crowded into the room but Michele wasn't with them.

A lean man, tall, with silver hair, whom Raine recognized as the man who played the part of the movie actor in the play, sauntered over to their table and looked down at Jade.

"Are you Michele's . . . husband?" There was a faint air of condescension in the words.

Jade's voice and face revealed nothing, but Raine's sensitive antenna reacted at once to the tension radiating from his body.

"Yes," he said softly. "Is there something—"

"Michele asked me to tell you she'd be delayed. She was sorry."

"Of course," Jade said politely.

"She should be here in twenty minutes or so. She rode with Tony, our director, and he wanted to stop off at his apartment and change clothes there instead of backstage as the rest of us did. Now if you'll excuse me. . . ."

Jade nodded, turned back, lifted his glass and swallowed the entire contents.

"Hey, brother, not so heavy on the Scotch. You gotta drive home, remember."

"I remember." The words were harsh. He got to his feet. "Do you two want another round?"

Stricken with her own pain, Raine gazed at him. "No. I don't want another drink."

Watching him stride across the room to get the drink that would anesthetize the pain, she felt helpless and angry. What a fool Michele was.

Beside her, Marc looked down into his drink. "That's not like him."

"No, it isn't."

"Maybe you were right."

She turned to look at Marc. "What about?"

"About leaving them alone." His grin was rueful. "I'm beginning to wish we weren't here. I didn't know things were so bad between them." Marc twisted the swizzle stick inside his glass. "Have you talked to Michele lately?"

She shook her head. "Not since she started driving to Canton every night for the play rehearsals."

She turned her head to gaze out at the water. Marc's voice came low in her ear. "There she is."

Michele, wearing a creamy, silk beige dress Raine had never seen before, came in the door. The gown outlined the mature curves of her figure, the high rounded beauty of her breasts. She clung to the arm of a darkly handsome man of medium height.

Michele was surrounded at once by members of the cast, and even from across the room, Raine could hear their effusive praise.

"You were marvelous, Michele, just marvelous. It's been a privilege to be in the cast with you. . . ."

And there, leaning with his back to the bar, stood Jade, watching.

Hardly knowing what she was doing, she jumped up. Like a guided arrow, she homed toward Jade. Halfway across the room, Michele's voice, newly resonant and precise, reached her ears. She turned to look at her sister.

". . . owe it all of course, to this darling man." Just as Raine reached Jade's side, Michele kissed her companion. It was not the obligatory peck of congratulation, it was an intimate kiss—a lover's kiss.

A silence fell in the room. The cast was strangely quiet, as if they were aware that another drama was being enacted. Several people glanced furtively in Jade's direction. His face was a dark, impassive mask. When Michele broke away from the man and laughingly told everyone to go have a drink, they began to move away from her toward the bar. Soft music radiated from speakers and people began to dance wherever they were, glasses in hand.

"Hello, Jade." Michele's voice was cool, confident. "You found us."

He didn't reply. He simply stood and looked at her.

His silence seemed to rattle her slightly. "Darling, I'd like to have you meet my husband. Tony Costelino, Jade Kincaid."

Neither man extended his hand.

Tony Costelino turned to Michele. "Have you told him yet?"

She gave Costelino a breathtakingly intimate smile. "I haven't seen much of my husband lately. Now is as good a time as any I suppose." She straightened slightly and fastened her violet glittering gaze on Jade. "I'm going to New York with Tony tomorrow."

Jade didn't move a muscle. In that low, controlled voice he said, "Is that supposed to surprise me?"

Michele laughed, throwing her head back and exposing the smooth, creamy line of her throat. "I should have known nothing surprises you. See, darling," she said to Costelino, "you've been worrying for no reason."

The other man frowned slightly, drawing his dark brows together. "Then you don't mind if your wife goes to New York with me, Kincaid?"

He couldn't quite believe that a man like Jade Kincaid would give up his wife so easily, Raine thought in stricken amazement. And, neither, somehow, could she.

Jade picked up his drink from the bar, tipped the glass and downed the contents. He replaced the glass carefully on the shiny wooden surface and then turned his head to gaze at Costelino. "She stopped being my wife the minute she walked in that door on your arm. You're welcome to her."

Raine stood frozen, unable to think of anything to say or do.

Michele had plainly not expected that. With a proud lift of her head, she said, "Does that mean you'll grant me a divorce?"

"I told you I'd be glad to give you a divorce."

Raine's mind reeled. *They had already discussed a divorce?*

In a bitter tone, Michele said, "As long as I agree to relinquish all visiting rights to Tate."

"You don't see him when you're here. Why should you worry about seeing him when you go?"

"I won't agree to those terms, Jade."

He shrugged. "If that's the way you feel . . ."

Michele turned to the man at her side. "Tony, be a darling and get me a drink. My usual."

Grasping Raine's arm, Jade said in a cold, deadly voice to Michele, "You'll forgive us if we don't stay."

Genuinely disconcerted, Michele protested, "But I thought I'd ride home with you?"

"Get Tony Darling to take you home," he growled. Raine caught a glimpse of the surprised expression on Michele's face. Then, in the next instant, Jade had grasped Raine's arm and half-dragged, half-pushed her past the people crowded around the bar. The bartender started to protest when Jade opened the door to the deck, but he took one look at Jade's face, closed his mouth and nodded his permission.

Outside, the cool breeze felt like heaven on Raine's hot cheeks. Starshine was reflected in the water and a sliver of moon had already traversed half the sky until it was overhead. She would have enjoyed the fishy smell of the water and the faint creak of the wooden steps under her feet had it not been for Jade, bearing down behind her, gripping her arm with steel fingers.

They reached the ground and Jade propelled her forward. What his destination was she had no idea. There was a patch of grass underfoot and a path that led to a double-width dock. Jade guided her toward it. Her heels clicked against the wooden dock, and she stumbled. Annoyed, she said crisply, "Are you planning to throw me in the lake instead of Michele?"

He stopped suddenly in the middle of the dock, his body as still as if she had shot him, his face a mask of anguish. Spasmodically, his fingers bit painfully into her flesh. An instant later, he dropped his hand and she was free. He moved away from her and, in a strained tone, said, "I'm sorry."

His face bleak, he turned away and stared out over the lake into the darkness.

Wrenching out the words past a throat that was tight,

she said huskily to his back, "If I could change things . . . if I could make the world move the way I wanted it to, I would never let her hurt you like this."

He pivoted round and took hold of her and suddenly she was in his arms, clamped against his lean body. "Shut up," he said fiercely. "Keep your damned sympathy. I don't want it."

"No," she said, "you don't want anything from me. Not even this—"

Driven by some dark force she could neither understand nor control, she pulled his head down to hers and captured his lips. He didn't respond, but he didn't push her away. After years of yearning to touch his hard, controlled mouth with hers, she could no more stop kissing him than she could stop breathing. She went on probing his lips with her own, reveling in the warm strength of the mouth that lay quiescent under hers. Oh, God, it was wonderful to feel his warm, beautiful mouth under hers. She had been waiting to taste it all her life. She circled his neck with her arms and pressed her body to his, knowing that this was the last time she would ever be this close to him, knowing that now that he had put Michele out of his life, he would want nothing to do with her sister, either.

"Kiss me back, Jade," she murmured against his lips. "Please, just this once. Kiss me. . . ."

He caught her long hair with his hand and pulled, not cruelly, just enough to make her tilt her head up to him fully. "Raine, my God, do you know what you're doing? Do you know what you're asking?" His grip tightened and she felt the aroused state of his body. The unfamiliar feel of him only heightened her own wild excitement. "Hasn't it occurred to you that I haven't been to bed with my wife for a long time? What makes you think I'd want to stop with a kiss?"

"I don't . . . I didn't think . . ."

His hands slid over her back, tightening, pressing her against him. The cradle of his hips nestled on hers, and even standing there in her clothes, she had the acute sensation that he was already making love to her.

"Well, start thinking," he said, lowering his head and kissing the soft skin of her cheek, making it impossible for her to think at all. "Start thinking about how I'd like nothing better than to take you home and make love to you until your body ached with it. Think about how it would feel to have me kiss every lovely inch of you." His mouth caressed the curve of her lips. "And think," he murmured into her mouth, "how wonderful it will be to wake up in the morning and know that what we shared was sex, not love, and that we can walk away from each other without either one of us giving a damn."

She recoiled as if he had struck her, but it was too late to escape. He locked her head in place with one hand, anchored her hips against his with the other, and kissed her with a tender passion that rocked her to the depths of her soul. His mouth sought hers as if it were a golden prize, his tongue playfully teasing under her lips, coaxing her teeth to open, plunging through with a flicking, tantalizing exploration of the dark honeyed sweetness she couldn't deny him.

Dying inside, she moaned softly, a wordless plea for him to release her. He only went on kissing her, cradling her even closer, seducing her with his mouth and his tongue and his hands. The hand that had held her head slid downward along her rib cage and swept up underneath her breast, searching for the swelling fullness that anticipated his touch.

Another soft, muffled sound of mingled pain and delight escaped her, and this time, he heard it. He let her go so abruptly that she was left lightheaded. One instant she was in his arms, and the next he was standing a foot away from her, the only sound in the night that of their ragged breathing.

In that cool dark silence, he said, softly, "Stay away from me, Raine."

She stepped toward him. "Jade, I—"

"Don't touch me." The words were like knives. A sob bubbled up and she turned to run from him. In violent repudiation of his own words, he caught her and whirled her around into his arms. Glittering gray eyes looked up at him, shining like silver gems. For a long, silent moment, he held her and gazed at her. Then he took a breath and expelled it, loosening his hold on her slightly. "Listen to me, you little fool. I told you to stay away for your own good. My God, you've handed me the perfect weapon of revenge, don't you see that? Of all the women in the world, Michele is most jealous of you."

She shook her head. "That can't be true."

"All right," he said in a strange, flat voice. "Add liar to my list of names, along with cuckolded husband. . . ."

"Jade, don't," she said in an anguished voice, clasping his upper arms.

He tightened his hold on her waist. "Listen to me. I'll say this just once and then I won't say it again. Stay away from me. Because if you don't"—even in the shadowy night she could see the dark, primitive glitter in his eyes—"I might throw away the last scrap of integrity I have . . . and take what you're so willing to give."

3

━━◦∞∞∞∞∞∞∞◦━━

It had been two weeks since Michele had packed her bags and left, two weeks of listening to the community buzz with gossip, two weeks of fending off questions and turning aside curious probings. She knew that Jade was saying nothing at all. She had the misfortune of walking into the little grocery store one afternoon and hearing Mrs. Denton say, ". . . silent as a tomb that man is, not saying a word. He's left to raise that boy alone and it's a disgrace, I tell you, a disgrace. Of course, what could you expect from those girls—both of them growing up without parents and Julia with her ideas of independence. . . ."

"Hello, Mrs. Denton," she said sweetly. The woman's face flushed and she muttered something about having to go.

That was only one of many incidents. Alternately, Raine seethed and suffered. When Julia announced that she would have a birthday party for Raine as usual, Raine protested, but her protest fell on deaf ears. Julia's eyes burned with defiant pride. "We're not going to become hermits," she said staunchly and marched out into the kitchen to begin writing out her list. Raine knew the subject was closed.

She spent the next few days working feverishly on the

paper, trying to block the coming event out of her mind. But on the night of the party, she dressed and came down the stairs with her head high. Julia's pride was infectious.

Most of the people Julia invited came. Laughing, already in a party mood, a dozen couples crowded into Julia's little living room where the rug was thrown back and the punch bowl set up on a round table. There were a few friends from Raine's high school days, a salesman she'd gotten friendly with since working on the paper, and a new couple who had moved into the community to escape the city. Raine smiled and greeted them, forcing herself to act natural for Julia's sake. After a while, she forgot Michele, forgot Jade. She drank Julia's rum punch, laughed and talked with people and danced with Marc.

But as the evening wore on, her laughter became strained and her mouth ached from smiling. Her facade was cracking. Dancing in Marc's arms, she let her eyes wander to the doorway. Jade stood there, his eyes fastened on her.

Stunned, she stopped dancing. Her feet were no longer connected with her brain. "What's wrong, honey?"

Marc turned. When he saw them break apart, Jade began to walk toward them with that lazy, controlled gait. Marc turned her slightly, cradling her possessively in his arms.

Twin stars of glittering anger burned over her. Then Jade's lashes came down and his voice was so cool and contained that she wondered if she had imagined that fire. "I'm sorry I'm late. One of the steers jumped the fence. Happy birthday." In the astounded silence, he leaned over and brushed her cheeks with his lips. She stared at him, trying to collect her scattered wits. Jade looked at Marc. "Enjoying yourself, brother?"

Marc stiffened. "As a matter of fact I am."

Julia came to their rescue. "Jade, how nice you could come. Have some punch." Julia linked her arm in Jade's and led him away. Marc turned her roughly into his body and pulled her close. In her ear, he muttered, "Why the hell did he have to come?"

"I don't know. I suppose Julia asked him."

Marc danced with her in silence for a moment and then said harshly, "He doesn't want me to marry you, you know."

Ripples of shock went through her. Why? Why? Staring over Marc's shoulder at Jade smiling at Julia and lifting a delicate glass cup to his lips, she said in a carefully light tone, "He probably thinks one faithless Taylor woman in the family is enough."

Marc's arms tightened around her. "Everyone knows you're not like Michele."

Her laugh was short, mocking. "Do they?"

She'd had two cups of punch and she was beginning to feel it. She felt lightheaded, reckless. She closed her eyes and tipped her head back, letting her hair fall down her half-bare back to the top of Marc's hands. Aware at once of her surrender to the sensuous pleasure of dancing, his arms locked her in a possessive hold. What was he thinking? She didn't care. The music would keep her thoughts away. The music would enclose her in a bubble where nothing mattered. Marc's touch no longer mattered, the music no longer mattered, her life no longer mattered.

As if someone had said her name, she felt the command to return to reality. Her eyes flew open. From across the room, Jade's eyes bore into her. They moved over her face, down the swinging length of her hair. Clinically, coolly, they traveled up again, along the path of her slim, bare arms looped around his brother's neck. There, in the crowded room, with people milling about and Marc's warm, moist breath at her temple, from across the room Jade mouthed silently, "I want to talk to you." She stared back, unable to believe he was saying those words to her. He frowned, commanding her to acknowledge his message. Woodenly, she nodded her head. The tension went out of his face and body and he turned back to Julia. He said something to the older woman. She nodded and he put his punch cup on the table and walked out of the room. He didn't look at Raine.

She pushed against Marc's arms. "Let's take a break, shall we?"

Marc leaned away to grin down into her face. He looked slightly dazed. "It is kinda stuffy in here, isn't it? Want to go outside?"

"That isn't where I wanted to go," she drawled.

His tanned face reddened. "Oh, sorry. Did you drink too much punch?"

"Something like that."

"You don't have to be bashful about . . . things like that with me, Raine." She wanted to laugh. It was his face that had turned a bright pink.

"Would you . . . let go of me?"

His face even brighter, he dropped his hands. "Sorry, sweetheart. I'm being inconsiderate." He looked into her face, his eyes adoring her. "It's just that I love you so much I hate to let you go."

She didn't love him—because he wasn't Jade. But she was fond of him. She leaned forward and kissed his cheek. He reached out, grabbed her shoulders and pulled her close, making her regret her moment of contrition. Irritation swept over her. She wanted to go and see Jade and hear what he had to say to her. Her body screamed to be loosened from Marc's possessive hold.

Palms on his shoulders, she pushed gently. He released her at once, grinning. "Save me a dance when you come back?" His smile was endearingly pleading.

"Of course," she whispered.

She detoured through the kitchen, but instead of turning left, she turned right, walked through the back porch and stepped out into the dark summer night.

It had been a warm, rainy August day and the air was

moist. From dark corners beside the house, crickets chirped, incessantly optimistic. What do they know?

The moist dew made the grass slippery under her high-heeled sandals. She walked away from the house, the light cotton of her dress swirling around her legs. Instinctively, she headed for the arbor, a latticed shelter shaped like a wedding trellis that gleamed white in the dim light from the street lamp. The town itself was quiet with that special tranquility that only small towns seemed to have.

He stood just outside the arbor. His tall, wiry form moved, and a thousand clamoring nerve ends came awake inside her. She stepped closer, aching to lean against his body and loop her arms around his neck just as she had Marc's.

"I ought to wring your sweet little neck."

Each word cut like a knife. Her head came up, her eyes glittered. She didn't have to ask what he meant. She knew. "What business is it of yours who I marry?"

He reached out and gripped the opposite side of the arbor, wrapping lean fingers around it, as if holding the narrow lathe would keep him from strangling her. "You made it my business when you put my brother in your sights."

The night breeze moved her hair and caressed her cheek. It was a breeze as soft and sweet as a lover's touch . . . and it made her ache with loneliness. "I didn't plan to murder him."

In the still, silent night, with the smell of roses in the air, his voice had a violent edge. "There are other kinds of deaths besides the obvious one. There's the living hell a woman can give a man. . . ."

"If you wanted Michele to stay, why didn't you tell her so?"

"What I wanted wasn't important. It was what she wanted that mattered."

"You still love her." Her voice seemed isolated in the warm summer air.

"I'm no longer capable of loving any woman," he said harshly.

"Is that why you don't want Marc to marry me, because you've been hurt?"

His hand whipped off the arbor and clamped on her shoulder. "I don't want you to marry Marc because I don't want him to go through what I'm going through."

His fingers were like steel, bruising her, but she braced herself and didn't try to move away. "If I do decide to marry Marc, I'll never leave him."

"You'll leave," he ground out harshly, his fingers doing the impossible, tightening even more, "there's nothing to hold you here. I'm amazed you didn't leave long ago."

Her body spun out the sensation, gave her a glimpse of what it would be like to be held in Jade's arms one more time. The thought made her crazily reckless. "I'll never leave here," she whispered huskily. "I belong here . . . just like you do."

"No woman belongs here. This is a man's country." The suppressed violence echoed in the air.

His disturbed cry only fueled her need to break through his prejudiced thinking. "But if a woman loves a man . . . she stays."

"And you love Marc enough to stay?"

Unable to lie, equally unable to tell the truth, she hedged. "I . . . haven't decided yet."

He met her hungry gaze with a fierce light burning in his own eyes. In the next instant, he pulled her into his arms with a hard, masculine force that excited her. "You don't love Marc." Tangling his work-roughened hands in the long silky strands of her hair, he held her half-away from him while his eyes probed her face with an intensity that she could see even in the dusky light. "You love me, don't you?"

It was an accusation that cried for denial. Uncowed, she flung her head up and faced him squarely, pride and courage evident in the taut line of her head and shoulders, her eyes lit with a liquid fire of their own. "How could I love you, Jade? You're bitter and hurt and you push me away whenever I come near you."

He murmured, "Not so very long ago you offered me consolation. Is the offer still open?"

Denial, sharp and acid rose in her throat. Yet she heard the soft word as it came out of her mouth. "Yes."

He stared at the creamy outline of her throat, the smooth perfection of her skin bared by the brief sundress, the defiant challenge in her eyes. His own body stiffened, and he groaned and clamped his arms around her in a velvet vise, dragging her close to him. "I don't love you," he said raggedly. "I can never love you. . . ."

His lips were like satin, smooth and faintly scented with Julia's rum punch and utterly wonderful. Unlike the night she had kissed him by the lake, this time he was the aggressor, and she reveled in the glorious wonder of being the object of his passion. He kissed her with an expertise that took her breath away. He commanded, retreated, enticed, controlled, demanded, retreated again to induce a more fervent response from her. He played on her mouth like a master violinist and she was all fire and light for him, singing in the resonance he created. He lifted his mouth slightly. "My God," he breathed the words warming her lips. "I've been thinking about doing this for days . . . and it's better, much better than I imagined it would be. . . ." He took her mouth again in a hungry possession and she responded, letting his mouth and tongue intensify her own growing hunger.

Abruptly, he pushed her away. "I swore I wouldn't touch you," he said in a voice of loathing, whether for her or himself, she couldn't be sure. For both of them, perhaps.

She felt an urgent need to be away from him, to hide. She stepped into the shadowed shelter of the arbor. From the safety of the dark arch, she whispered, "I'm not ashamed of what I feel for you." She turned away and wrapped her hands around her middle, feeling the brush of a rose leaf.

A sound came from his throat, a low guttural moan that might have been ripped from his vocal chords. "For God's sake, Raine, don't say any more."

Pride kept back the tears. "I'm sorry if I've embarrassed you or made you uncomfortable. There isn't anything you can say to me that I haven't said to myself a hundred times or more. I . . ." She lifted her chin. "I'll get over it." Lies, all lies. She had loved him since she was sixteen without a single sign of encouragement from him. How could she possibly forget him now that she had tasted his velvet kiss?

"Raine?" Marc's voice sailed through the night. Through the leaves of the climbing rose vines, she could see him framed in the square of light from the door. "Raine, are you out there?"

Startled, they both froze. Then Jade stepped behind her and folded his arms around her waist, pressing his body into hers, making their two shadows one inside the leafy arbor, his urgent possession a silent command to be quiet.

She entered into the conspiracy, letting her body merge with Jade's and holding her breath.

"I guess she's not out here, either," Marc's rueful voice said to whoever was behind him. There was a moment more of silence. The door closed with a soft swoosh and they were left there in the arbor with only the sound of their breathing, now suddenly ragged, and the sound of the crickets.

Then she became aware of other things, the feel of Jade's tall lean body against her back, the comfortable cradle of his arms . . . and the undeniable evidence of his arousal.

She moved, wanting to be away from him before the wanton thoughts that had possessed her a moment ago flared up again.

"Don't move," he ordered roughly. "Just let me hold you."

The husky intensity in the words sent a white-hot fire

racing through her. "Jade." She whispered his name and the sound trembled into the night like a butterfly in first flight.

He drew in a quick, tortured breath. "My God. Don't say my name like that."

"I'm sorry . . ."

His hand wandered, tracing the supple line of her rib cage. "You should be sorry. You have a whole list of sins," he murmured, "a sinfully sweet body, lips that are smiling instead of petulant, eyes that are honest and open, hair so long I could get lost in it. . . ."

"Jade, don't. Oh, please don't . . ." Her heart was tearing, ripping into little shreds.

"Do you know how long it's been since I've tasted a woman's skin?" The husky question sent a ripple of shivers through her. He dropped his head to the side of her neck and lifted her hair to nibble. His warm lips against her skin increased the sensual ache to an intolerable level.

"Jade, don't . . ."

He laughed softly and brushed her hair with his lips. "Console me, Raine. Make me forget. . . ." His hand moved up to explore her rib cage. The sensuous feel of his hands and the agony of wanting him to cup her breast completely made her cry out in desperation, "Jade, I . . . I didn't mean . . ."

He touched her shoulder and with one quick move, he brushed her strap down over her arm. Her fears, her anxieties were swept away by the heat of her excitement. Her skin was on fire, her body and mind whirling with excitement. He turned her in his arms and bent his head to the soft flesh just above the rounded curve. She was powerless to resist him. This was Jade holding her, caressing her, pressing his hot mouth against her skin. This was Jade making her blood sing in her veins. Fantasy and reality coalesced into a starburst of forbidden dreams. The unfamiliar charge of desire exploded from deep within her. "Jade, no—"

Against her skin, he murmured, "Yes." His mouth moved treacherously close to the dusky nipple. She had read about the delights of a man's mouth on a woman's breast, but until this moment, she had never felt the agonized pleasure of velvet lips on her own smooth roundness.

Her mind echoed his words as if he had whispered them in the night breeze, *I can never love you.* "Let me go," she whispered. "Jade, please let me go. . . ." His hand cupped and supported her breast and his tongue came out and caressed the rosy tip. ". . . Oh!" Her sharp exclamation brought a soft chuckle to his lips. His hands tightened at her back, steadying her to receive the deeper possession of his satin mouth. Driven by a longing that had her fingers digging into his shoulders and clinging to him for balance, she called on the one name she knew would break the spell. "Michele—"

His tongue stopped its slow, erotic course and his head lifted, shadowing her anguished face. In night air heavy with the scent of roses, the sound of their quickened breathing rasped in counterpoint, his a deep dragging in of air, hers shorter gasps that shook her pale, bare flesh. Flesh that cried out at the loss of his touch. "You're still married . . . to Michele."

A sound—a low, heavy, agonized sound—issued from his throat. He twisted away and walked out into the night. She was left alone in the arbor, alone with the crickets and the fragrance of roses and the shadows. Alone with the breeze that caressed her bare breast in a pale imitation of a lover's touch.

"Kiss him," Marian, Tim's wife, chanted, her pixieish freckled face alive with impish pleasure, her spoon clinking against the glass. "Kiss him, Raine."

They were sitting around the big oak table in Julia's dining room. Only Marian and Tim and the Kincaid men had remained for the after-party coffee. Julia sat at the head of the table and smiled at them as they drank her

47

leftover punch, ate the last pieces of cake, and talked and laughed in easy companionship.

White cake crumbs clung to the corner of Marc's mouth. Jade sat across the table from Raine, the mocking smile on his mouth sending a dagger of pain through her.

The tapping, clinking sound beat into her brain. "Come on, Raine." Marian's little-girl voice had taken on a touch of impatience. "Kiss him. Kiss Marc. Kiss him, Raine." A wicked grin lifted the freckled face. "You've got to get in practice for the reception."

Raine turned to Marc, thinking only of stopping that incessant beat of silver against glass, that needle-thin voice saying her name and Marc's in tandem.

His eyes lit up. Then his hands reached out and he grabbed her bare shoulders. At an awkward angle that had her head twisted nearly to the limit, he pulled her to him and pressed his mouth against hers. His lips were warm and moist, a boy's lips and heavily scented of sweet vanilla frosting and rum. She tried to move away, but he had her shoulders in a hammerlock grip. Driven by his own fantasies and the rum in Julia's punch, he boldly deepened the kiss, thrusting his tongue against the barrier of her teeth. His flesh was moist, intrusive, unwelcome. She pulled and twisted in his arms, and this time he let her go, but he smiled possessively at her, his cheeks red with a triumphant flush. Her anger and annoyance increased. No longer able to look at him, she turned away and her gaze slammed into Jade's. In the depths of those green eyes, contempt gleamed, a contempt that seared her, but was carefully hidden from anyone else by the mocking smile that tilted the corners of his mouth.

It was a fencing match and she was losing. His contemptuous scrutiny seared her face, nicked her cheeks, her mouth—the mouth that she had offered to him—and then to his brother, all within the space of an hour. Whatever scorn he felt for her, her own matched it.

How could she marry his brother after she had tasted Jade's kiss?

"Now, Raine, as soon as you decide on a date for the wedding, let me know. There'll be a million things to do." Julia's voice, low and husky, delightfully feminine, sliced through the nightmare.

"It won't be for a while," Raine said, wondering where the conventional words came from.

Marc's hand covered hers. "Why? We don't need to wait."

Raine said coolly, "We don't need to rush, either." As if it were a beacon, she felt Jade's gaze sharpen and hone in on every inch of her face.

Marc said, "Speak for yourself, honey." He lifted his palms up and leered at her.

A bright red color fired the skin in her cheeks. "Marc, stop being such an idiot. You've had too much punch."

"We're not even married yet and she's already a nag."

"That's something to think about, brother."

Julia's reaction was immediate. "Jade, don't try to scare him. Raine isn't the type to nag and you know it."

"No," Jade drawled, "she doesn't say anything. But she has a vocabulary of eloquent looks."

Laughter rumbled around the table. Only Raine knew that Jade's words were double-edged.

Later, when everyone had gone home but Marc, he coaxed her to come out and sit in the porch swing with him.

"Now, isn't this cozy," he said, pulling her close with the arm draped over her shoulder.

"Very traditional," she murmured.

"Smell the roses."

She did, and thought of Jade.

"Love is in the air," he said softly. He started to kiss her, but she pushed at him gently, keeping him at bay. She knew she couldn't endure another evening like this one, with everyone thinking she and Marc were a permanent couple. In a voice soft with regret and remorse, she said the words that she would have given anything not to have to say. "Marc, I . . . I can't marry you."

He pulled away and even in the dark, she could feel his puzzled eyes traveling over her face. "Why not?"

"It's just that I . . . I can't." In desperation, she launched into the rehearsed speech. "We're good friends, Marc. We've been good friends for a long time. But being good friends doesn't mean—"

"Can it, Raine." The words seemed harshly unreal coming out of Marc's mouth.

"What?" She stiffened and tried to regain her emotional balance.

"I said can it!" He got up from the porch swing with a force that sent it creaking back and forth even with her still in it. He thrust a hand through his blond hair and went to stand by a pillar, his face away from her, his profile lit by the street lamp. "I might have known it was too good to be true."

"Marc, I—"

"I told myself you really do love me. But you don't, do you?"

"Marc, you're a good friend . . . maybe that's part of the problem. Maybe we're too . . . comfortable with each other. I don't love you the way . . . people thinking of marriage should. I—"

"And besides," the words were blunt and cold, "now that your sister's gone, you've got a clear shot at him."

Sick with shock, she whispered, "I don't know what you're talking about."

He turned and took a step toward her. "You know what I'm talking about."

She fought to control her voice and her face. "Don't stand there and make wild accusations that have no basis in truth. . . ."

He took a step closer. "Oh, they have a basis in truth all right. The basis is my big brother, the lady killer. Jade

Kincaid, the macho stud of Verylon High." Under the words a deep current of jealousy vibrated, a current Raine had never known existed. Marc threw back his head and laughed—a harsh, unpleasant sound. "I thought it would change when he got older. But it didn't. He's over thirty years old and you're still gone on him, aren't you?"

"He's only thirty-two. You make him sound as if he's got one foot in the grave. And as for my being 'gone' on him . . . don't be ridiculous."

He crashed down on the porch swing beside her, catching her arm and forcing her against the corner. "I'm not being ridiculous, and you know it."

"You're jealous, Marc, and jealousy distorts people's views of reality."

"Was it jealousy that made me imagine I saw him with you in the rose arbor tonight?"

Shocked to the core, she stared at his dark face.

"You thought I didn't see you, didn't you? But I did. I knew you were there. He kissed you, didn't he?"

"I'm not going to discuss this with you."

His harsh crack of laughter made the words die in her throat. "Don't give me that sick little evasion. You were with him and he kissed you. Your lips were swollen when you came back into the house, swollen because they'd been kissed by a man who arouses you more than I ever have."

She sat stricken and chilled, listening to him, wishing she could deny his words.

"What's the matter, Raine? Can't think of anything to say?"

"Marc, please . . ."

"The hell with talking. I'd do better to take a lesson from big brother. . . ."

He bent his head suddenly and pulled her to her feet, covering his mouth with hers, smothering her words, kissing her with a strength and passion she didn't know he possessed. His mouth hardened on hers and his tongue entered her mouth and ravished cruelly, taking all, giving nothing. She pushed against him with a strength born of fear and panic. He made a low, animal sound and released her, watching her as she sank back against the hardwood swing, her breath coming in short gasps.

In the cool, damp dark night, he stared at her. "I wish you luck with him," he rasped. "He was faithful to Michele for six years and that's a record for him." He peered into her face, a mocking twist on his mouth. "I think he loved her once. But he has something else in mind when he looks at you!"

4

Outside the print shop, the winter wind whistled, driving gusts of snow up the main street of Verylon. From somewhere outside, the slam of a door penetrated the air thickened with snow. The sound hit Raine's ears with the force of a gunshot. She jumped, her nerves jangling. It was the screen door flapping on Harry's Bar and Grill across the way. Winter or summer Harry never took the door off. The person who let it bang shut moved away from the protection of the building and climbed into his car.

Raine gave up trying to edit the galley sheet spread on the desk in front of her and looked at the clock. Ten-thirty. Harry's customers were going home. As she should be.

She stared out into the snowy night. The screen swung on its hinges for another moment before it finally settled into place. The car backed up, disappeared into the white haze. She went on gazing at the winter scene framed in the large plate glass window, mesmerized by the play of snowflakes as they danced in the air. The wind gusted, swirling snow from the overhang into a graceful pirouette with the flakes falling from the sky. Red and green lights on the little tree she had set out in the street glowed through the filmy veil. With this storm, they would have a white Christmas. The thought brought no joy.

She picked up the paperweight on her desk and shook it. Artificial flakes drifted over the *fleur de lis* in a microcosmic echo of the world outside. The tiny dots of white floated and settled. It had been almost five months since her birthday, five months since she'd talked to Jade. Oh, she'd seen him from a distance of course. And once, she'd gone into the drugstore and he'd been there, talking to Sandy Tremain. She'd said hello, and he'd answered in that low, male voice and immediately turned back to Sandy. She'd felt the pain for days afterwards.

To fill the empty, aching spaces of her life, she'd thrown herself into working on the paper. They'd picked up some new subscribers in the area and four new advertisers. She hadn't seen Marc, which was not surprising since he never came into the print shop the way he used to do. He was avoiding her. She didn't blame him. She understood the unwillingness of the Kincaid men to see her—even though their reasons were entirely different. She understood but that didn't make her loneliness any more bearable. She had lost three of the most important people in her life at the same time. She was isolated, and very much alone. She couldn't confide in Julia. She had no one.

She rubbed her eyes and tried to focus on the work in front of her. She was proofing the story she had done on the school cheerleaders. There was a picture with the article. Krissy, Kim, Anne, Candi, Heather and Emma grinned at the camera, but unfortunately Kathleen Miller had been hidden behind the double tier of the pyramid. It was the first year Verylon had been represented at its games by a group of girls who were both willing to spend endless hours practicing and agile enough to perfect ambitious routines like the pyramid.

Crack! The slap of the door sounded again, and again Raine jumped. She made a soft moan of resignation and reached in the bottom drawer of the desk for her purse and the headache tablets she carried now as a matter of course. Shaking two out of the plastic bottle, she got up to walk past the Linotype machine and the press to the little room partitioned off at the back where there were amenities for living: a cot, a sink, a two-burner hotplate, a small refrigerator, and behind what looked like a closet door, a toilet and sink. She drew a glass of water and swallowed the tablets. The cot looked soft and inviting nudged up against the wall with the quilt Julia had made for it. How good it would feel to lie down, just for a minute, to help the tablets work.

She turned off the harsh overhead light, slipped off her shoes, and lay down. But even from behind the extra wall, she could hear the sound of the door across the street as it slammed once again. She moaned, closed her eyes and pressed her fingers against her forehead, trying to rub the pain away.

Another sound filtered through the pain—but it wasn't the door of the bar and grill. It was the door of the print shop, its little tinkling bell banging against moving wood. A blast of cold air told her she wasn't imagining things. She had a visitor.

A chill shivered over her skin, not entirely from the change of temperature. There was absolutely no reason why anyone with legitimate business would come into the print shop at ten-thirty in the evening.

Her heart pounded. Swinging her feet to the floor, she told herself she should have locked that door. It simply hadn't crossed her mind. She wished now it had. She was frantically trying to thrust her feet into her shoes when a sound made her look up.

The light from the desk lamp in the other room threw a halo around her unexpected caller's head and body, giving him shape and substance. She didn't need to see his face to know who he was. The wildly accelerated beat of her heart told her.

Jade said, "What are you doing?" His voice was soft, slurred, that faintly puzzled tone totally unlike him.

He hadn't even asked who sat there in the shadowy darkness of the cot. He had known it was her and he had known exactly where to look for her.

She was no longer afraid; she was angry. What right did he have to stalk in there like a shadowy giant in his sheepskin jacket and scare the life out of her? "What does it look like I'm doing? I'm trying to get my shoes on."

"Are you ill?" He took a step into the room, and her heart reacted with an even more frantic bumping against her ribs. The soft concern in his voice was muzzy. Had he been drinking? She'd heard he was making a visit to Harry's a nightly ritual lately.

She said coolly, "I was proofreading and I got a headache." With a sense of relief, she finally slipped her feet into her shoes. Fully shod, she stood and faced him, fastening her eyes on the dark shadow of his head, knowing that the light was reflecting off her face and making it easier for him to see her than the reverse.

She took a step toward him. The faint odor of alcohol told her he had been in Harry's for more than a ham sandwich. She said, "From the smell of you, I don't think you're in any condition to be worrying about me. You'd better go home, Jade, while you can still find the road."

"I've been worrying about you," he muttered inexplicably.

"Why should you be doing that?" She longed to see the expression on his face, but she couldn't.

"I've discovered I don't like playing God."

Faintly alarmed by the intense tone of his voice and the stillness of his body, she moved closer to him. "What on earth are you talking about?"

"Marc has asked Sandy Tremain to marry him."

His words were so far from anything she had imagined, she was speechless. He stood stock still, waiting for her reaction. Time hung in a curious suspension. She stared at him, the dark figure in an open jacket, hard, tough, lean and male, with flakes of snow melting in his amber gold hair.

He said, "If you still love him, I'll stop the marriage."

Her mouth lifted in a wry smile. "I thought you were tired of playing God."

"I . . . owe you that much."

She sighed. "You don't owe me anything, Jade." She added dryly, "I'll send him a punch bowl."

He said something under his breath. Knowing that stress and an excess of alcohol had driven him to offer her this weird apology, she chided, "You've had too much to drink. Come on, cowboy, you need some fresh air."

She tried a push to get him moving. Her palm slid past his open jacket and connected with his chest. His reaction was immediate—and violent. He caught her arm and swung her around opposite him, pinning her against the side of the doorframe with a strength that both astounded and terrified her. She had thought him sloppily drunk, easy to handle. She'd miscalculated badly. She stared up at the profile of his face, seeing the hard determination, the gritty agony of a man driven to the limit. His other hand grasped her waist in a grip of velvet steel. She wore a pullover sweater and heavy denim pants, but the material was no barrier to the warmth and weight of his hand. Against her hip, his palm fit as if it were the mold she'd been poured from.

"Don't you care?" he muttered.

"About Marc? No. Why should I?" Her breathing quickened.

"I thought you loved him," he murmured, his voice soft, as if he were thinking about it, "but you didn't, did you? You're as incapable of loving a man as your sister was."

That stung. Her voice bitter and arid, she replied,

"Well, now that you've discovered the truth about me and eased your conscience, I know you'll sleep better tonight."

"I'd rather be sleeping with you," his voice was a low, seductive murmur poured into her ear.

Startled, she reeled with shock. She fought her reaction to his seductive words with anger—and the biggest lie of all. "I'm not . . . interested in you, Jade."

"Do you know what happens when you tell falsehoods?" He tapped the end of her nose lightly, chuckling. Then he pulled her closer and pressed his mouth to her forehead. "You're lying, honey. You melt in my arms when I kiss you. Your mouth is deliciously pliant when you open it under mine. I can feel how much you want me every time I hold you."

Her skin burned. She forced her voice to steadiness. "You do have a colossal ego, Jade. Let go of me."

He shook his head. "I could have walked out of here if you hadn't touched me." He closed his eyes and lifted his hand to her cheek. His knuckles bent, he grazed the backs of his fingers over the smooth, satiny skin, raising fire. "But now," he breathed, his voice soft as thistledown, "now it's too late." His caress explored her cheek until he uncurled his lean fingers and cupped her chin. "Tell me you hate having me do this to you."

"Jade, stop it." Her voice was breathless, huskily soft. "You don't know what you're doing."

"Don't I?" He laughed softly and shook his head. "I'm doing what I always want to do whenever I get within fifty feet of you. . . ." His words dissolved her resistance. She felt his hand slide around her nape and hold her head steady. Breathless, she waited for his mouth to complete that long, slow descent toward hers.

His lips were cool and scented with alcohol. He kissed her sweetly, like a boy wooing a girl on her first date. For a long tender moment, he made no move to deepen the kiss. He simply held his mouth on hers, as if the contact gave him a deep satisfaction he wanted to savor. Then he groaned a low sound of pain and pulled her deeper into his arms. Under the open edges of his coat, he locked her in his male world, a world redolent with the aroma of good clean skin, alcohol, leather and wet wool. The lips that had been so gentle against her mouth now claimed her with a fierce possessiveness that heated her blood as it consumed her. His tongue probed, sliding enticingly over hers, exploring corners, dropping depth charges that resounded in the deepest, most feminine core of her.

Electric excitement raced through her veins and encircled her body, making her giddy. He lifted his lips. But as if he couldn't bear to break the contact with her skin, he dragged his mouth along a path from her cheek to her temple and buried his lips in her hair. She clutched at his back and nuzzled her face into his chest, feeling the warm strength of him everywhere, against her cheeks, her body, her palms. She wanted to melt into him and take away the pain he had suffered—and was still suffering.

She stood in his arms, feeling the overwhelming release of her love. She belonged here. She always had, since the beginning of time.

His hands moved. Suddenly, he swept her upward, lifting her off her feet and cradling her against his chest. Stunned, she looked up into his face, seeing nothing but a shadowy form and the dark hollows of his eyes. Peace vanished, panic took its place. The lovely feeling of being one with him washed out on a tidal wave of fear. The man who had picked her up like a woman he was carrying away to ravish was a stranger to her.

She lifted her head away from the heavy suede of his jacket. His breath fanned her face. Though he had been drinking, the hard strength in his arms and body never wavered. Some inner force drove him.

A primitive instinct told her not to betray her fear. "Jade, put me down." Her voice was crisp, cool and practical. "You'll hurt yourself. I'm not a featherweight like Michele. . . ."

"No," he muttered, "you're not Michele."

Fighting the agony of hearing his wife's name dragged out of him, she kicked her feet against his arms and stiffened her body, hoping he would loosen his hold on her. He didn't. He tightened his grip and walked the two steps to the cot. When he lowered her to the soft quilt that was still warm with the heat of her body, she took a breath and half-raised herself up, pushing against him. He came down heavily on top of her. She resisted, writhing against him, knowing now beyond a shadow of a doubt that he had something far more elemental than simple comfort on his mind. The struggling movements of her body only sharpened her senses and made more vivid the feel and warmth of him. His hard masculine chest against the softness of hers exploded the guards she had built around her long-buried love.

She made a sound of protest and he eased away from her but did not let go of her. He merely held her with one hand and shrugged a shoulder out of his sheepskin coat. He reversed the process with his other arm, and the coat went sliding to the floor.

Her heart throbbed in her ears, blood pounded in her brain. *Jade*, her body whispered. *No*, her mind answered. *Not like this. Not like this.*

He leaned over her and her veins throbbed with desire. He wore a black turtleneck jersey with his jeans and she braced her palms against the cotton-covered strength of his chest and said in a mixture of excitement and fear, "Jade, listen to me. This is impossible. You . . . you've had too much to drink."

He chuckled and buried his mouth in the side of her neck, nuzzling the warm cavern under her ear, his lips discovering the roundness and texture of the soft lobe. "Not to worry, sweet. What you do to me is too damn strong to be blocked by a couple of shots of Scotch."

"Jade, no, listen to me, please. I can't let you—" He stopped her words with his mouth, claiming the inner recesses with his tongue, his body shifting over hers, the evidence of his male arousal telling her he was absolutely right about his ability to drink and still make love to her. She burned with excitement and struggled against it. She couldn't let him kiss her into mindless submission.

He lifted his mouth and she knew this was her last chance to stop herself from surrendering completely to him. Appealing to that streak of innate chivalry she knew he had, she called on her acting ability and gasped a protest. "Jade."

"What is it?" His mouth wandered over her throat.

"You're too heavy. You're hurting me."

He lifted up at once. "I'm sorry, honey. Where did I hurt you? I'll kiss the ache away." With one smooth movement, he raised her sweater and fastened his warm mouth on her bare midriff. Without any recourse to acting ability, she gasped. He laughed softly, his breath fanning her skin. He pushed her sweater away and those devastating lips ascended ever closer to the warm curve contained in the silk of her bra. When his mouth touched the soft underside of her curved flesh, she gasped again.

"What an innocent you are."

"I'm not . . ." Why she was denying it, she had no idea. She had never exchanged intimacies with Marc like this. The few times he had made a fumbling pass at her, she had laughed and knocked his hand away. She wasn't laughing now. And she wasn't pushing Jade away. . . .

"Lift your arms," Jade murmured in her ear.

"No . . ." As if she hadn't said the word, he picked up her arm and freed it from her sweater. In one deft move, he had the sweater over her head and off her other arm. Cool air wafted over her skin. Caught in wanting him to look at her and knowing she shouldn't allow it, she twisted her head to one side, a small moaning sound of protest coming from her throat. With unerring precision he placed his lips on the soft triangle where the sound vibrated.

Against her throat he murmured, "Don't be shy, sweetheart. You're beautiful. God. So beautiful." He breathed the words against her skin huskily, his lips feathering over her. "Let me look at you." He slid his hands under her, undid the clasp of her bra, untangled her arms from the straps and tossed it aside. She shuddered and clasped his back, knowing that her resistance was weakening. His mouth teased her, played with the fullness of her rounded curve without touching that delicate, taut center. She moaned again, this time with need. Buried in her mind, those stolen moments with him in the arbor surfaced, and she shook with the anticipation. She wanted to feel his mouth on her naked skin again, his lips and his tongue moistly caressing her.

He strung out the agony, exploring her breast from every direction, the side, the top, underneath, while his other hand played tantalizingly over her other breast.

"You don't want me to do this to you, do you, Raine? I can almost hear that mental battle going on inside your head. And yet you can't stop me. You love the way I make you feel."

"No," she murmured. "Jade, let me . . ." she wasn't sure what she was going to ask him to do, but he stopped her words and all coherent thought by taking the dark burgundy center that ached for his touch into his mouth. Her instant shuddering reaction made a ripple of sexual excitement drive through his body. Her excitement fed his, and his fueled hers. They were caught in an endless spiral of pleasure given and received. She lifted her hands to his head and clasped his nape. The flicking motion of his tongue drove her into a primitive state that was sheer bliss. She was all femininity, the perfect receiver of his masculine adoration. Totally in his control, she was terrified—and yet exalted. Everything he did to her was so right, so right . . . for he was in her power, too. Each caress, each touch of his hand, each soft love word murmured against her skin told her how much he enjoyed touching her, stroking her . . . pleasuring her.

The torturing ecstasy of his mouth left her. He pushed up, pulling out of her arms. She lay back, stunned by his leaving—until she heard the soft tinkle of the bell on the front door.

In an instant, he was on his feet, his body filling the doorway as it had before, but facing the office. His bulk shielded her from the eyes of whoever had entered the print shop.

"Jade?" It was Harry's voice. "What are you doing here?"

She huddled in the covers, barely breathing.

"Turning off lights the women left on," Jade said without hesitation.

There was a silence, as if Harry was mulling that over. Then he said, "You okay?"

"Yeah, I'm okay."

"I was closing up and I saw your car. You'd had a few and I—"

"I'm okay," Jade said more forcefully. "I'll be leaving in a minute."

Harry's voice had a reluctant note. "I can drive you home . . ."

"In this storm? Don't be a fool. My pickup has chains." Another silence. Then Jade's voice, cold and commanding. "I'm okay, Harry. Go on and close up."

Harry agreed reluctantly, and the bell tinkled again.

She sat up, clutching the quilt around her, her blood pounding. On a nervous half-laugh, she murmured to the form in the shadows that had turned back to her, "Do you know what happens to little boys who tell lies?"

He came and sat down on the bed beside her, smiling, his hands on her shoulders pressing her back. "There goes my fine Irish nose." His smile deepened and his eyes sparkled. "Should I have told Harry the truth?"

She could see him clearly in the light stream from the other room. He was smiling down at her, his attractive lips curved upward. "No. Harry would have had a heart attack."

Jade chuckled. "Maybe not. Harry's lived a long time.

It would take a lot to surprise him." He leaned over and kissed the soft skin above her breast.

"Jade . . . please. I . . . he might decide to come back in a minute to see why you're not leaving."

His warm mouth traveled over her avidly. "Come home with me, Raine."

She fought the clamor in her body to say yes and said softly, "No, Jade."

He lifted his head. "Just . . . no?"

"Just . . . no."

"Do you have a reason or is teasing men a hobby of yours?"

Anger swept through her like a hurricane, but she tightened her control and said coolly, "You're a married man, Jade. And you're married to my sister."

His eyes swept over her naked shoulders. "That didn't seem to bother you a moment ago."

"A moment ago I . . . wasn't thinking too clearly."

He cursed softly, sprang off the bed and went out into the other room.

She tried to dress quickly, but her hands were shaking and she had trouble fastening her bra. At last, fully dressed, she left the darkness of the rear of the shop and walked into the light. He sat on the edge of the desk and stared out the window into the night storm, much as she had been doing minutes ago.

He turned, his hooded eyes telling her nothing. "I'll take you home."

"It isn't that far. I can walk."

Through gritted teeth, he said, "Don't push me, Raine."

He turned out the lights and, while she locked the door, he slid into the pickup and started the engine.

The air was icy cold inside the cab, but at least she was out of the wind. Her short ski jacket wasn't enough for the sub-zero temperatures and she shivered.

"You'd better take a hot bath when you get home."

"So had you," she shot back.

In a cool, mocking tone, he said, "I was thinking more in terms of a cold shower."

She had no answer to that.

In front of Julia's house, he stopped the pickup, the chained wheels crunching on the snow. She found the door handle with her cold fingers.

"Sleep well, Raine," he said with ironic mockery.

Matching his tone exactly, she said, "You too, Jade."

After Christmas, the whole town buzzed with the news that Marc Kincaid and Sandy Tremain were getting married on Valentine's Day. Sandy came into the print shop and ordered invitations, her attitude toward Raine a mixture of interest, defiance and wariness. She assured Raine, with much satisfaction Raine thought, that both she and Julia would receive an invitation.

"Are you going?" Julia asked on the next Tuesday night. They were seated at the kitchen table drinking hot cocoa and munching on the popcorn Julia had made in a small celebration of New Year's Eve.

Raine said carefully, "Of course, why not?"

Julia stared down at her cup. "I've never wanted to be an interfering, prying aunt, but—"

"I'm very happy for Marc and Sandy," she said firmly. "Sandy has adored Marc for ages." She looked into Julia's worried face and smiled, her eyes open and honest.

Julia gazed at her for a long moment, as if assessing her words. Then she looked down, stirred her chocolate and laid the spoon carefully on the table. "You haven't been yourself since before Christmas and I wondered. . . ."

"Winter always gets me down." She tightened the muscles of her face and kept her smile lifting her lips.

"Are you going out with Doug tonight?"

Raine nodded and relief relaxed the tense lines in Julia's face. "He's coming around ten and we're going to see a midnight movie. Something about intrigue on a Greek island. We thought all that sunshine would cheer us up."

"Does Doug need cheering up?" Julia's eyes fastened on her face.

Caught, Raine said frankly, "Probably not as much as I do. But it has nothing to do with Marc."

Julia turned to a philodendron that stood on a small stand next to her chair and absently fingered a leaf. She loved plants and had them everywhere in the kitchen, on shelves in the window, on tiered stands next to the telephone. They spilled out into the living room and decorated the end tables on either side of the couch. "It wasn't a very happy Christmas for any of us. I thought Michele would call again. Do you know if she's been in touch with Jade?"

Raine shook her head. "No. I haven't talked to him since . . . in quite a while."

Julia didn't seem to notice Raine's slip. "Surely Michele sent Tate something for Christmas. I wonder if Tate liked that wooden tractor and combine set you got him."

"He called yesterday." Raine smiled. "He told me he liked it. He sounded so grown-up on the phone. He must have practiced what he was going to say."

Julia's mouth took on that firm look Raine knew well. "I don't want to lost contact with that boy. You shouldn't, either."

Raine rose from the table, picked up her cup and went to the sink to rinse it. "I don't intend to."

"Then perhaps we should decide to visit on a regular schedule."

Raine turned around, leaning back against the counter for support. "A regular schedule?"

"If Michele were here," her mouth tightened momentarily, "she would probably see him on weekends. We could take her place. If we took turns, it would only be every other weekend for each of us."

She wanted desperately to say no. Constant, regular

exposure to Jade was the last thing in the world she wanted. But to refuse would be churlish. It would also break Julia's heart. "That sounds . . . reasonable. I don't know if . . . Jade will—"

"I'll talk to him about it," Julia said firmly, getting to her feet. "I'll call him right now while I'm thinking about it."

"I'm going up to get ready," Raine said, giving in to her urge to escape.

Later that evening, sitting in the movie theater beside Doug, she regretted the impulse that had led her to accept his invitation to go out on New Year's Eve. He was a paper salesman, and had grown up in Canton and lived in South Dakota all his life. He was dark-haired and tanned and had a keen sense of humor, and he had made frequent visits to Julia's shop, perhaps more frequent than necessary. He had come into the shop the day after her disastrous evening with Jade, and he had made Raine laugh with his crazy anecdotes. When he had suddenly asked her to go out with him on New Year's Eve, she had said yes.

But now, sitting beside Doug, letting him hold her hand, her thoughts were filled with the night she had sat beside Jade in a dark theater and had been so aware of him that she heard him breathing. Throughout the movie, and even later in the pizza parlor when Doug joked with the waitress, she seemed caught in limbo, suspended between two worlds, the real one where Doug's grin shone at her, and the fantasy world inside her head where Jade commanded every thought and memory she had ever had.

She got through the evening without, she thought, betraying herself too much. But when Doug pulled up in front of Julia's house and put the car in neutral, he turned to her and said, "Happy New Year, Raine," and pulled her into his arms and kissed her. She could no longer pretend. She stiffened immediately and pushed herself away.

He dropped his hands from her shoulders at once. "Has this thing with your sister turned you off men?" Doug was friendly, and people talked to him. He knew most of the gossip in each of the towns he visited on his route.

"No," she said. "It's just that—"

"There's someone else," he finished the thought. That was not what she was going to say. But it was the truth, she thought ruefully.

"I . . . just don't want to get involved seriously right now."

"Hey," he said, lifting his hands in a palms up gesture, "neither do I." He grasped the steering wheel and looked out into the street. Snow had begun to fall, a fine light snow that filled the air like white mist, making Julia's house and the rest of the town look like a setting out of a Currier and Ives. "I'll see you next week, okay?"

"Fine," she said, fumbling for the door.

"And Raine."

Tensing, she turned back. "Yes?"

He perused her strained face slowly, the expression in his eyes unreadable. "If you can manage it, use more paper next week, will you? Sales have been falling off."

Her laugh was instantaneous and relieved. "I'll do the best I can, Doug."

When he came in a week later, she asked him to be her escort at Marc and Sandy's wedding. He grinned and said he'd enjoy eating wedding cake with her, even if it was somebody else's.

5

Daddy, can we go home now?"

Jade looked down at his small son and smiled. Tate was dressed in a gray tuxedo with a pearl silk cummerbund that was the exact duplicate of the one he wore. "Not quite yet, son. We have to eat some wedding cake."

"Is it chocolate?" Tate asked hopefully.

Jade shook his head. "We're on short rations this afternoon. It's white cake."

Tate shifted his feet and looked out over the crowd. He's already learned to hide disappointment, Jade thought wearily and silently cursed himself for marrying a woman who had taught his son the meaning of disappointment and loneliness at such an early age. Tate fought it valiantly, but Michele's rejection colored every facet of the boy's life, Jade knew. He was his old self only after a day spent with Raine.

He'd agreed to Julia's persuasion and allowed them to set up a visiting schedule with Tate. He wasn't quite sure why he had given in so readily. Maybe because he knew she spoke the truth, that Tate did need to know there were women around him who cared for him. Jade hadn't been enthralled with the idea at first, giving Tate over to Raine and Julia every Saturday, but when Tate came home, so obviously happy and anxious to share with

Jade the details of his exciting day, Jade knew he couldn't rescind his decision. The die was cast.

He'd thought Sandy would be a good influence on Tate, too. But for some reason Tate was wary of Sandy, even though she tried very hard to understand the boy. She'd insisted that Tate be included in the wedding party so he'd feel a part of things, and even in the hubbub of today, she'd spared a moment to speak to Tate and tease him out of his stage fright. In her radiant happiness, Sandy spilled affection over everyone. Marc accepted her love with a foolish grin on his face. Jade's lips moved in a cynical smile. He only hoped Marc had better luck with marriage than he had had.

He ran a finger around under the tight collar. What a day. The wedding had been at a small country church, but after a picture taking session that nearly had Jade crawling the wall, the wedding party had driven back into Verylon. The reception was at the Legion Hall, a barn of a building that was roughly the size of a small airplane hangar and had the same ambience. Someone had tried to decorate it and had almost been defeated by the task. They had solved the problem by tying red and white crepe paper streamers to the backs of the chairs and suspending a huge pair of paper, accordion-pleated doves from the ceiling. Above the heads of the guests, the doves moved lazily in the heated air, their plump breasts bumping in inanimate affection. In the corner of the room, a group of musicians played romantic songs. The whole atmosphere clawed at Jade's nerves. He wanted nothing more than to go home, pull the tie from his throat, get out of the idiotic rented suit he wore and stop smiling.

The room was filled with the scent of roses and the heavy smell of cigarette smoke and coffee brewing, yet somehow out of that mixture of aromas, he caught the whiff of a delicate scent he had never forgotten.

"How are you holding up, Tate?"

It was Raine, just as he knew it would be, slender and

70

lovely in a blue silk dress he couldn't remember seeing her in before, squatting down in front of Tate, reaching out to straighten the small tie that didn't want to stay level. Behind her stood a man, a dark-haired man he didn't know. The man smiled down at Tate. "Hi, tiger. You knocked 'em dead in the church this afternoon. I've never seen anyone carry a ring pillow with such style."

Tate smiled up at the man, obviously familiar with his teasing. As he smiled back at the boy, the man's hand dropped to Raine's shoulder in a gesture of possession. Involuntarily, Jade's hands clenched at his sides.

"It was okay," Tate said. To Raine, he said wistfully, "Have you had cake?"

Raine smiled. "Hey, listen, you're the privileged character. You're in the wedding party. I won't get mine until you have yours."

Tate stared back at her with Michele's eyes. "Why can't I have mine?"

"You have to wait until everyone has some punch and says hello to your uncle and your new aunt." She poked the pearl cummerbund with a delicate, pink fingernail. "Are you hungry? Maybe I can steal some mints and nuts for you off the punch bowl table."

"He isn't hungry," Jade said softly, staring down at her head, taking in the silky perfection of her golden-brown hair as it lay in shining waves halfway down her back. "He wants to go home."

Raine straightened and the action drew his eyes down the length of her slender figure. The blue silky thing clung in all the right places. Was she going all out, dressing up for that clown she was with?

"You haven't met Doug Martin, have you, Jade?" God, her voice sounded different when she said his, Jade's, name. Did she hate him for what happened that night? She had a right to. He'd had too damn much to drink. He'd stopped going to Harry's after that. "Doug, Jade Kincaid. Tate's father."

Doug Martin smiled a broad smile that irritated Jade

and stuck out his hand. "Glad to meet you. I've enjoyed getting to know your boy."

Tate had told him Aunt Raine's "friend" had taken them both to a movie in the afternoon last weekend. He hadn't liked it then, and he didn't like it now. He took the man's hand, said his name and nodded coolly.

Raine stepped close to him and said in an undertone, "Doug and I can amuse Tate for a minute if he's getting bored."

He didn't need a strange man entertaining his son. "He's all right."

Tate, sensitive to every nuance in his father's voice, glanced at him in surprise. He hadn't missed what Raine said. "Why can't I go with Aunt Raine, Daddy?"

Jade gave Tate a bland, mocking look. "I might get frightened, standing here all by myself."

Raine's eyes flashed over him and the normally guarded expression dropped away for an instant, revealing a raw emotion, that, before he could decide what it was, vanished. He stared at her, wondering what it was she had felt so strongly it had made her eyes go molten silver. With those eyes and that hair streaked with gold, she was easily the most attractive woman in the room.

The emotion vanished. She withdrew, went behind a barricade, her voice coolly polite as she said, "Natalie Forsyth asked about you a moment ago."

He had gone into the bank the day after that episode with Raine, and Natalie had smiled at him with such obvious appreciation and suggested casually that they spend New Year's Eve together. He'd agreed—and cursed himself later for it. Natalie had been pleasant enough, but he simply wasn't interested in her. He'd almost forgotten about that one night out, until now. Obviously, the Verylon grapevine was in good working order. He should have guessed he was at the top of the interest list. But Raine scrupulously avoided gossip, he knew that. Both she and Julia tried as much as possible to squelch rumors. Then why this veiled reference to Natalie? Unless, God, was she still nursing a remnant of that adolescent crush she'd developed on him when he first married Michele? She couldn't be. He'd done everything he could to crush it, even making her believe he'd have loveless sex with her. He didn't want her damned devotion. Love was a cruel joke. Maybe it worked for other people but it didn't work for him.

"If it's all right with you," Raine's frosty tone brought him back to reality, "I'm going to take Tate out into the lobby to get him a soft drink out of the machine."

"Go ahead," he muttered, wondering how much of his thoughts he had betrayed by the look on his face.

Raine took Tate by the hand and led him out of the smoke-filled room. He found a wall to lean against and later, when she came back guiding Tate past the scattered chairs and tables with one hand and carrying a bright red can of soft drink in the other, he tried not to watch her. But his eyes didn't obey instructions. Raine settled Tate and herself at a table and offered Tate the container of pop. After he had taken a few sips, she engaged the youngster in a complicated hand-clapping game that required concentration and coordination, and Jade gave up the struggle to look elsewhere and openly watched them.

A sing-song kind of chant went with the hand-clapping and Raine's soft voice was mesmerizing. Tate concentrated fiercely, his mouth open, his eyes on Raine. They made a picture that could have graced any magazine cover, the slim, beautiful woman sitting knee to knee with the enthralled boy-child.

"Jade?" It was Sandy in her frothy swirl of white silk. "We're going to cut the cake. Will you propose the toast?"

He was the last person in the world to do that, he thought grimly, but he nodded, and when the ceremonial moment came, he simply said, "To Sandy and Marc. Long life and happiness," and lifted his glass.

At the moment he put it to his lips, his eyes met

Raine's. Even though she was several tables away, he felt the pull of those silver eyes again, and the deep-felt emotion in them. She had raised her glass, and the lovely curves of her slender body strained against the blue silk. His body responded, desire stirring deep within him. He tipped his glass, blocking her out of his sight, draining the alcohol into a throat that had gone dry.

It was abstinence that was making him feel this way. He hadn't had a woman in his arms for a long time, not since the last time he had held Raine.

He wanted to hold her again. Not stopping to think, driven by a need he didn't want to analyze, he put his glass on the table and began to thread through the crowd toward her.

"Jade?" A hand plucked at his sleeve. "Hello. I've been waiting for a chance to tell you how devastating you look."

The petite, red-haired woman smiled up into his face. She was wearing a low-cut dress and she had positioned herself close enough to give him an unhindered view.

"Hello, Natalie. How have you been?"

"Missing you," she said in a soft voice. "Why haven't you come in to see me?"

"I've been busy," he said and knew the excuse was probably the stupidest thing he had said that day. And the day wasn't over yet. He went on talking to Natalie, saying God knows what and in the end offering to refill her wine glass. The moment he left her, John Forsythe, her recently divorced husband, stalked over to her and began talking, his face a bright red. Jade glanced at them and decided Natalie could wait for her wine.

Raine was sitting alone, holding a sleepy Tate on her lap, swaying back and forth with him to the music.

"Where's Martin?" He slid into the chair next to her.

"He had to leave."

"Here, let me have him. He's too heavy for you."

Raine's arms tightened around Tate. "He's fine."

His son was half-turned in her arms, leaning between

her breasts, his head curled into her shoulder. He lay against her, snuggled into her soft curves like a tired puppy. He wasn't asleep, but his eyelids drooped. Something harsh and alien squeezed Jade's throat. "He'll wrinkle your dress."

She looked at him over the top of Tate's blond head, that silver fire flashing in her eyes. "I don't give a damn if he does."

His voice low and lethal, he ordered, "Give him to me."

Her arms tightened around him protectively. "My God. I never dreamed you could be this vindictive."

"Vindictive?"

"You can't stand seeing him in my arms, can you?"

In a blinding flash of clarity, he saw the truth. He was jealous, yes, but not of her. He was jealous of his own small son, lying so peacefully and comfortably . . . in the place where he ached to be.

A heat raced upward, beat against his nerves, tore at his insides. "Hold him all you like," he told her. Catching a glimpse of the surprise on her face, he rose from the chair and muttered, "I've got to get some fresh air."

He shrugged into his coat and let himself out the door. His warm breath made fog in the air as he bounded down the steps of the hall and strode past the frosty-windowed grocery store, past the feed store, past the park with a covered swimming pool. Barren trees sighed and mocked him, their branches scraping together in the slight winter breeze.

Suddenly he was out in the country. The pale, wintery sun was just setting, casting long blue shadows on the snowy landscape that swept ahead of him like a silvery ocean. Flat and level, covered with two feet of snow, his grazing land started here, just beyond that redwood fence. He needed to replace that fence. He'd have to do it before he turned the herd loose this spring. He had a thousand acres of prime land, and he wanted more. He wanted to double the acreage, so Tate would be assured of a place of his own when he was old enough to appreciate it. He'd borrow more money and buy more calves. Fiercely, he tried to concentrate on the future, tried desperately to keep away the truth. But the truth beat at the door of his mind until he had to let it in. He'd been jealous of his son . . . *jealous.*

My God, he was a colossal fool. Was he going to make the same mistake all over again?

He heard footsteps crunching on the snow behind him—someone running. He turned.

She wore nothing on her head, and she clutched the edges of her unbuttoned coat together at her waist. "Jade, wait."

She was the last person in the world he wanted to see at this moment . . . and the only one. He waited, watching as she huffed along the road toward him, her high heels sinking into the snow. She'd catch pneumonia.

"You're crazy to come out here like this. You'll freeze to death."

"I've got to talk to you." She was breathing fast from her exertion and her breath was coming in quick, little gray puffs into the cold air.

"Where's Tate?"

"Marc is watching him. Jade, I . . . I'm sorry for what I said back there. I know . . . I know it's been hard for you and I . . . I understand how you feel. I'm not trying to come between you and Tate. I would never do that. But I just can't let Tate grow up with your terrible prejudice against women."

"Is that what I have?"

In the soft sunlight, her eyes burned with earnestness. "You have a perfect right, I realize that. But all women aren't like my sister. She was never satisfied here. She shouldn't have married you."

"Tell me something I don't know." His smile was ironic.

She shook her head in mild exasperation. "Don't try to keep me away from Tate."

He gazed at her. "How long will your devotion last, Raine?"

"I don't know what you mean."

"Right now, Tate's an interesting diversion for you. But you've been seeing this . . . Martin regularly, haven't you? Suppose you decide to get married." He waited in a breathless silence.

"Suppose I do." She lifted her chin and above the dark fur collar, the line of her throat was creamy, enticing. "That doesn't mean I'll see any less of Tate."

In a quiet, deadly voice, he said, "He's a lifetime commitment, Raine."

She stared back at him. "I know that, even if my sister didn't. Stop linking me in your mind with her." Her voice was as frosty as the air around them. "We're not alike at all."

Her gray eyes glistened with defiant anger. He met her silvery gaze, fighting that electric sensation of sexual energy her close proximity gave him. "I'll try to remember that," he said softly.

For a moment, she looked stunned. Then the dark pupils of her eyes dilated, and for the first time, she seemed conscious of the cold. She shivered and wrapped her coat around her, her eyes never leaving his. She turned to go, her back straight, her head proud and high.

He wasn't conscious of speaking until he heard her name leaving his throat. In the frosty air, it sounded like a groan of pain.

Slowly, teetering a little on her high heels, she turned back. "What is it?"

He stood for another long moment, watching the way the wind took her hair and swirled it around her shoulders, molded her coat against the slender lines of her body. "Come here."

She hesitated for an endless eternity. Then she shook her head. "No." The word echoed in his ears as if she had shouted it when in reality her voice was huskily soft.

"I need to hold you." He heard his own words with a

kind of detached amazement. He had sworn he would never be vulnerable to a woman again. And here he was cutting his heart open for the sister of the woman who had betrayed him. It didn't matter. He needed her so much he ached with it.

"I can't . . ."

He didn't move. He wasn't going to move toward her or grab her. She had to come to him of her own volition. She had to want him as much as he wanted her. "Raine."

She cried, "Don't ask me. Don't."

"I . . ." he gritted his teeth. "I need you."

"You don't need me." Her voice trembled with the intensity of her emotions. "Any woman would do." Her eyes went molten silver.

"Listen to me . . ."

"No," she shook her head. "Don't try to lie to me. Michele has been gone for almost a year and you've done nothing to dissolve the marriage. I . . . I can't . . . can't get involved with you, Jade. I want a man who . . . who is free to love me for . . . for what I am."

Her silvery eyes played over him. He stood watching her, conscious that the sun had disappeared behind the edge of the earth and the landscape was more gray and bleak than it had been before. "Martin?" he asked, his mouth curling. "Is Martin your candidate for that honor?"

His caustic tone made her draw in a sharp breath. "Yes," she said finally, "yes." She turned away from him to walk down the snowy road with her head high, leaving him there to stare after her in the dusky light.

He spent a restless night. The next morning he picked up the phone and called the airport. "I want a seat on the first available flight to New York City on the seventeenth." After a slight delay he was told that his ticket would be waiting for him at the airline counter. His second call wasn't as easy. Raine's voice sounded casual and familiar when she said hello, but when he identified himself, her voice turned icy.

He steeled himself and said, "I wonder if you could take care of Tate for me for a few days."

There was that little pause of surprised silence. Then she said, "Yes, of course."

"I'd like to bring him in tonight if I may."

There was a slight pause, then she said, "I don't think that will be any problem. I'll get the bed in Michele's old room ready. I can take him to school in the morning when I go to work and pick him up in the afternoon."

"Good. I'll see you later on this evening, then."

All day, she'd felt it, the tenseness, the waiting, the uneasy anticipation. Jade had evidently taken her words to heart or he would never have asked her to take care of Tate. But where was he going in the dead of winter?

It was snowing again when Jade's pickup pulled up in front of Julia's house. Raine met them at the door, the tall lean man and the young boy with flushed cheeks and bright eyes who was excited about staying with Aunt Raine and Grandma Julia.

"I'll take the suitcase," she said, reaching for it, brushing his knuckles with her soft fingers.

He relinquished the case and watched her as she went up the stairs. She was wearing a dress, a fine wool one, in a soft beige color that brought out the gold in her hair. As she ascended the stairs, he could see the shapely curves of calf and thigh encased in nylon stockings.

Tate tugged impatiently at his hand. "Put the sled out on the porch, Daddy."

Julia insisted that he stay for supper. After supper, at the table surrounded by enough plants to fill a green-house, Jade sent Tate into the other room to play while they had their coffee and then drew a piece of paper out of his pocket. "There's the address and phone number of the hotel I'll be at in New York City." Raine's reaction was a sudden dark flare of color in her cheeks. Seeing her body betray her made his stomach tighten.

Julia recovered first. "You're going to see Michele?"

"Yes. Is there anything . . ."

Julia shook her head. "We hear from her occasionally. I don't need you to carry my messages." Julia's normally soft voice had a crisp edge. "Be careful, won't you, Jade? New York City is a big place."

"I'll be careful," he promised, unable to take his eyes off Raine. She sat very still and said nothing to him . . . not even goodbye.

He hated the city; he always had. Once before he had come East and then he had carefully put away his Western clothes and purchased a suit and a pair of tight-fitting shoes. This time, he said to hell with it, and when he checked into the Roosevelt Hotel, he wore his sheepskin jacket and his comfortable old boots. No one batted an eye at his clothes, except a couple of women who gave him admiring glances. Did they think he was a Texas rancher with oil wells to support his cattle operation? God, he wished he was.

Installed in his room, he looked around. From the window he could see only a concrete well created by the walls of the buildings surrounding the hotel. Vertical lines all of them, and to a man accustomed to scanning the wide expanse of the prairie, it was like being locked in a prison.

He turned away, a soft growl of disgust escaping him and reached for the phone . . . then stopped. He'd be a fool to give Michele advance notice. He knew where she was rehearsing. She hadn't hesitated to tell him during one of their brief telephone calls. She'd called to ask about Tate and had given him the address and telephone number where she could be reached. He suspected that it was Costelino's apartment. He no longer cared.

He looked at his watch. Two o'clock. He'd wait until later in the afternoon, toward suppertime. He flung himself down on the bed and stared up at the ceiling. He wondered what Tate was doing. Thank God he didn't have to worry about him. Raine would take care of him. Raine loved the boy as much as he did. Raine . . . images poured through his mind. Raine at sixteen, staring up at him indignantly, her denims torn from the barbed wire fence she had followed him through. Raine on the back of a horse, looking like a graceful young animal with her incredible hair flowing out behind her. Raine with Tate sleeping against her breast.

He grimaced, feeling the tension in his shoulders, his back, his thighs. He had to relax, get control of himself. He would need all his wits to bargain with Michele. God, how could he have been so wrong about her? Ironically, it was that wild, restless quality that had attracted him to her in the first place. She'd seemed so alive, so vibrant. When she told him she loved him, he'd thought his life was complete. But the first winter they were married the weather was severe even for South Dakota. They'd had two weeks of bitter cold, and almost eighteen inches of snow fell. The blizzard confined them to the house. He had tried to console her. He'd carried in wood for the fireplace, gone into the stock of wine, wooed her on the dreary winter nights when the wind howled around the house. At first, she'd enjoyed the lovemaking but as the days went on and their isolation continued, she became irritable and petulant. When she discovered she'd become pregnant, she was livid with rage. It was then that he'd begun to love her less. By the time she left, he felt nothing for her. She had borne his child, but she didn't love Tate. She was incapable of loving anyone— and she had damn near robbed him of the ability to love anyone as well. In his pain and rage, he'd lashed out at Raine . . . his body tensed. Hell! This was getting him nowhere. He'd go out and find a coffee shop and stay there until it was time to go to the theater.

He'd expected a theater, not a church—except that it was unlike any church he had ever seen. There were boards where the stained glass windows should have been. He squinted at the old sprawling building tucked in between two high-rises. The steeple was painted a bright, robin's egg blue. "Are you sure this is the right place?"

The cabdriver bristled. "This is the address you gave me, buddy. Either pay the fare and get out or I start the meter going again."

Jade handed him the money and got out.

Inside, the floor creaked under his booted feet. The entryway was a mauve color, a sort of pinky-lavender that smote the eye. He followed the path of a plastic runner over the dark blue carpeting and came around the corner to what must have once been the sanctuary of the church. The altar area had been expanded and converted into a stage. Michele was on it, saying lines that made no sense to him.

A burly man, obviously the watchdog, rose out of the wooden seats. "Sorry, buddy. Nobody's allowed to watch rehearsals." He took a step toward Jade. He was Jade's height and forty pounds heavier.

Jade stood his ground. "I came to talk to my wife." He nodded in Michele's direction, his cold, stony tone matching his adversary's.

Michele stopped and looked out from the stage. He could see her straining, trying to see from the lighted stage into the darkened hall. From a seat about a third of the way back, Tony Costelino rose.

Jade stood, meeting Michele's gaze, his hands clenched. It was a danger signal and Michele knew it.

After a long, loaded silence, she said in a casual tone, "Let him stay, Matt. He won't bother me."

From his place in the empty row of seats, Tony shook his head. "We'll take a break. It's time, anyway."

The other actor on the stage shrugged his shoulders and moved away from Michele. She turned and disappeared in the wings. A second later, she appeared at a doorway on the side of the stage. She walked gracefully up the aisle, stopping beside Costelino and linking her arm in his. Even with all her bravado, she needs his support, Jade thought, marveling at his own ability to coolly analyze the actions of a woman he had once loved.

"You're a long way from home, cowboy." Her voice had changed. She'd only been gone a matter of months, and she was like a creature from another planet.

"So are you," he drawled.

She smiled at him, a feline, amused smile. "No. I'm more at home here than I've ever been anywhere in my life. I belong here."

He thought that was probably true. "I'm glad." At her arched eyebrow, he said, "I'm only here because you left a few ends dangling."

"Did I? What ends?"

Jade's eyes moved over Costelino. "Is there anyplace where we could talk?"

Costelino took Michele's arm and unwrapped it from his. "Go on and talk with him. I'll go back and see if I can figure out what's wrong with that microphone."

"Sit down." She gestured toward an aisle seat. He looked at the hard chair and said, "Isn't there a place where we could get a cup of coffee?"

"Across the street. Are you buying?"

"Yes, of course," he growled.

The coffee shop Michele led him to was clean; it had highly varnished table tops and shiny glass cases filled with rolls that reflected his own grim face back to him. He got coffee in plastic cups and carried it over to the booth she had slid into.

She lifted the cup to her lips. "I assume there's nothing wrong or you would have called."

"You might ask how your son is," he said through gritted teeth.

Over the top of the cup her eyes flashed. "What difference would my asking make?"

"To him, none." He shrugged, his shoulders moving under the heavy jacket.

"I can't be hypocritical, Jade."

He stared at her. She had her own peculiar brand of honesty which was as much a part of her as her creamy skin and her graceful way of moving. But it was an honesty that didn't appeal to him. She was a stranger, a beautiful stranger, with nothing to offer a man but the beauty of her body.

"Don't you think it's hypocritical to be married to one man and living with another?"

Her eyes flew to his and in a fleeting instant, he saw the quick, feline assessment of his mood. When he leaned back against the bench lazily, she laughed, a release of tension. "So you know." Her eyes flickered over him. "What are you going to do about it?"

His tone was dry, ironic. "I thought I'd do the decent thing and divorce you."

She laughed again. "Be my guest."

"You agree?"

She leaned back, more at ease than she had been a moment ago. "Of course. As long as you grant me visiting rights."

A muscle in his jaw moved. "What kind of visiting rights?"

"Two months in the summer," she said without hesitation.

"No."

"Those are my terms." She shrugged. "If you're not willing to meet them . . ."

"Who's backing your play?"

He watched while she toyed with her spoon. "What do you know about backers?"

"I'm a cattleman, in case you've forgotten. We're the biggest gamblers around. I know about having to borrow upfront capital to realize money on a long shot."

Dark eyes looked up at him from long lashes. "Are you saying you'd be willing to invest money in the play?"

He watched her sultry eyes rove over him. Once that blatant invitation had fired his blood. Now he felt nothing. "How does fifteen thousand dollars sound?"

Michele said, "In return for relinquishing my visiting rights? Not enough."

He gritted his teeth. They were bargaining over his son and his feeling of revulsion grew. "Twenty thousand?"

"Make it twenty-five," she said smoothly, "and you've got yourself a deal."

He didn't flicker an eyelash. "I want a signed statement from you before I hand over the money."

"You'll have it. Tony has a friend who's a lawyer." She stood up. He followed, angling his body out of the booth with a lithe easiness that concealed his tension. "I'll be going over it with a fine tooth comb," he warned her.

"You won't have to," she said sweetly. "I wouldn't want visiting rights if you gave them to me, Jade. I knew you'd come across if I held out long enough."

His eyes burned down over her. He was furious, not because she'd tricked him, but because she cared so little for their son. For a long moment, he gazed at her, his eyes traveling over her petite body. How could he have been so blind? "What makes you think I won't rescind our 'agreement' now that I know the truth?"

"You won't," she said airily. "You're a man of your word, Jade, one of the few left around. Maybe that's why I married you. After my parents died, I didn't have much stability in my life." She slanted an eyebrow. "I thought it was what I wanted. I didn't realize being secure would bore me to death."

He threw a bill on the table and turned away, no longer interested in anything she had to say. But at the bottom of the four steps that led out to the street, she caught his arm. "So now you're free, Jade." Her fingers tightened. "You know . . . I hate to see you spend the night in New York alone. Why don't I . . . " she framed the words carefully, watching him, "go back to your hotel with you?" She smiled. "Just for old time's sake?"

He steeled himself to keep from showing the revulsion he felt. "Just for old time's sake what, Michele?"

She murmured, "Do I have to say it? Darling, you're a

very attractive man. Seeing you like this . . . I remember how very good you are in bed. I want you, Jade."

"And that's supposed to impress me?"

She looked at him, her eyes pleading. "If you were anything else but a rancher . . ." She linked her arm in his just as she had Costelino's a moment ago. "I'd never have let you go, darling."

His stomach squeezed in revolt. "Go back to Costelino, Michele. He's your best bet now."

She pulled away and stared at him, her eyes blazing. "You're glad to be rid of me, aren't you? You can't wait to go home and console yourself with my little sister."

He shook off her hand, the tautness of his arm telling her she had hit exactly on target. "Leave her out of this."

"But she's very much in it, isn't she," Michele shot back.

Deliberately, he turned his back on her and walked into the wintery night, thinking that anything Michele said or did no longer mattered to him. If he'd been thinking clearly, he would have known better.

The next morning, in Tony Costelino's apartment, the tiny alarm next to the bed went off. Irritable and not remembering, Michele mumbled a succinct word and reached for the clock. Why in God's name . . . she came awake suddenly, remembering why she had set it. She reached for the phone, moving carefully so she wouldn't disturb Tony.

The phone seemed to ring for an interminable time. But she let the rings go on, knowing that Raine would have to get out of bed and walk down the stairs. Julia had never installed an upstairs telephone even though Michele had begged and pleaded for one.

At last the ringing stopped. "Hello?"

Raine sounded sleepy and vaguely muddled. Perfect.

"Hello, Raine." She made her own voice sound heavy, sleep-filled. "Jade wanted me to call you and tell you he's on his way. He'll be in Sioux Falls around one o'clock this afternoon." She laughed huskily. "He over-slept and almost missed his plane."

There was a long silence, and when Raine did answer, her words were husky. "Did he?"

"Yes." Michele yawned noisily into the phone. "Oh, God, there's the maid. I told Jade to put out the 'do not disturb' sign but he must have forgotten."

Michele heard the slight intake of Raine's breath followed by a long, humming silence and smiled. Then she said in a solicitous tone, "Is Tate all right?"

"He's fine." The gritty answer made Michele's smile broaden.

"I'm glad. Well, have a good day, Raine. Look for me in the papers."

Another long silence. "Raine?" Michele was sweetly concerned. "Is anything wrong?"

"No. Was that all you wanted? My feet are getting cold."

"That was all. Goodbye, Raine."

Michele hung up the phone and rolled over. She ran an experimental fingernail down the spine of the man who lay with his back to her. He wasn't sleeping; she knew that. Costelino rolled over and grasped her by the nape of her neck, slipping a hand between her head and the pillow. "What the hell are you up to, you little cat?"

"I'm having my cream and eating it too," she said smugly.

"You little bitch," he said with a mild, mocking affection. "You're almost too much for any man to handle."

"Care to try?" she said softly.

"I'll do more than try," he growled and pulled her close for his kiss.

Raine watched as Tate stuffed his things in his suitcase, the teddy bear he said he didn't really need but had brought along because he didn't want Teddy to be lonesome, the red pajamas with their rubber feet worn thin, and two sets of T-shirts and jeans. His mouth held in serious concentration, Tate worked on folding his shirts. His pale gold hair shone in the light as he bent over the bed. His features, still round with baby softness, had that handsome symmetry that would make him a good-looking man one day. A man who looked like Jade. He would resemble his father and have the added attraction of those dark, searching eyes that her sister had bequeathed him.

Dully, she felt the stab of pain. She had been in a curious limbo all day, not thinking, not feeling. She knew that when the shock wore off, the pain would be intense.

What had she expected? Not that, surely. What a fool she was. Jade had a perfect right to make love to Michele. She was, after all, his wife. Raine was the transgressor. She had no claim on him at all. And yet . . . when he took her in his arms, it felt so right, so good. Memories arose. She shut them away, knowing they would bring nothing but pain.

"I'm done, Aunt Raine." Tate looked at her with little-boy satisfaction.

Raine forced her mouth to smile. "Want me to help you close the case?"

"Yes, please." Even after only eight months of Michele's absence, his constant exposure to Jade had made him gravely serious, far too polite for a boy of five. Raine snapped the suitcase closed, and knew that no matter what happened, she wasn't going to lose contact with Tate.

The waiting seemed endless. Tate ran to the door a dozen times, looking for Jade. Raine had tried to interest him in the television program Julia was watching, but he wouldn't sit still long enough to get interested in the show. She was almost ready to go into the kitchen and pop some popcorn just to give Tate something else to think about, when she heard the car pull up. Tate heard it too and bounded to the door. Raine remained where she was, standing in the arched doorway that led to the kitchen.

Seeing him—tall, infinitely male, his amber gold hair dusted with snowflakes, beaming down at Tate and then swinging the boy up into his arms—was like glimpsing in a store window a diamond she wanted but could never have.

"Did Aunt Raine take good care of you, son?"

Tate nodded. "We went to see Tom Cannon's puppies. Can I have a puppy, Dad?"

Jade shot an amused, mocking glance at Raine. "I have the feeling I'm being set up," he said softly, smiling.

She couldn't answer his smile. "Maybe you are. Tate could use a diversion right now."

"He isn't the only one," he said softly, smiling, thinking she would understand.

To his utter amazement, she went pale and her body stiffened. "I thought that was what you went to New York for."

"Jade." Julia came out of the living room, smiling. "I didn't know you were here. Will you have a cup of coffee?"

Grappling with the implication of Raine's words, and forced to control himself in front of Julia, he said in an even tone, "No, thanks, Julia, not this time. I'd better get tiger here home and in bed. Tomorrow's a school day." His eyes flickered over Raine and the anguish he saw in hers alarmed him. Did she really believe he'd gone to New York to amuse himself with Michele? My God, she had to know him better than that. He'd taken that trip to get his life straightened out so that he could come to her with a clear conscience. But now, just as he was on the verge of clearing the tangled mess of his life, she stood looking at him with this agony. His head ached with travel fatigue and a sense of impending disaster. "Thank you for taking care of Tate," he said wearily to Raine.

"He was no trouble." Her cool tone told him nothing. "Any time you want to go . . . away . . . I'll be glad to keep him for you."

He met her eyes, his own guarded. "I don't think I'll be

going anywhere again soon." And with that, he turned and left, knowing he would have to wait to talk to her until he could catch her alone.

It was two o'clock the next afternoon, just after Julia had gone home, when the bell on the door of the print shop began its familiar jangle. Had she been unconsciously waiting for the sound of that bell all day? She must have. She forced her eyes up from the press. It was Jade, wearing his heavy sheepskin jacket and jeans and a dark green sweater that matched his eyes. His cheeks were red with cold but his eyes glowed with determination. Knowing he wouldn't be put off, she shut down the press and self-consciously wiped her inky hands on a rag she kept near the press for that purpose.

"Did you want something?"

He came into the room, closer to her, and she instinctively leaned against the bookcase at her back.

"Several things actually," he said softly. "But an explanation would do for a start."

"There's nothing to explain." She turned away and started for the desk, hoping to put the broad oak surface between them, but before she could reach safety, he stepped in front of her, all six-foot-two of his lean body barring her from her desk.

"I think there is. I'd like to know what you meant yesterday."

She lifted her head and faced him, her eyes blazing. "You know exactly what I meant."

He reached out to grab her arms, but when her eyes filled with revulsion and she shrank away, he stopped his hands in midair, clenched them and thrust them in the pockets of his jacket. A low sound of pain escaped his throat. "Why are you so sure I spent the night with her?"

"She called me from your hotel room."

"How do you know? Did you talk to a switchboard operator?"

"No, but she said the maid was coming in—"

"Anybody can say a maid is coming in and make you

believe it . . . particularly a talented actress." The temper he held in control colored his voice.

She met his eyes, watching the dark green irises turn the color of the sea. "Jade, do you realize how incredibly stupid this is? You don't have to apologize to me for staying the night with your wife."

"I'm not apologizing, dammit. I'm trying to get you to see the truth."

"You're the one who needs to see the truth!" It was a cry from the heart.

He clenched his fists more tightly. It galled his soul to defend himself to her. "The truth is whatever you're willing to believe."

She said quietly, "No. The truth is that you still love her."

"Whether I know it or not," he said in grim, satirical agreement.

"Something like that."

"Do you really believe I could go from your arms to hers?"

"Jade, I'm the other woman. Michele's your wife."

"Not anymore." He wanted to tell her that his "wife" was living with another man, but it would only be an added burden for Raine to carry. Michele was her sister.

"She'll come back, Jade. She'll have her fling at acting and she'll find out how hard it is to break in and she'll come back. And you'll want her again."

"That's not true. Raine, listen to me. . . ."

She shook her head. "No, don't. I don't want to hear any more."

Jade hunched his shoulders and she had the uncanny feeling that he was trying to ward off some pain.

Annoyed, he stared at her. He'd be damned if he'd go on trying to convince her he was no longer emotionally involved with Michele. Maybe she had a reason for doubting him. Maybe she didn't believe it because she didn't want to. Maybe she'd fallen in love with Martin and thought this was an easy way out. He was making a fool of himself. She no longer cared about him, that was obvious. Dammit all, what was the use? He swung around and strode to the door, yanking at it so fiercely that the twine looped over the little nail broke and the bell came loose from the door. Clinging and clanging, it dropped to the floor and rolled in front of his booted feet. While she watched in frozen silence, he picked it up with great care and put it on her desk. Fingering the tattered pieces of hemp, he said, "I'll bring some rope in from the ranch and fix it tomorrow."

"Don't bother," she said huskily. "We always have lots of twine around."

His head bowed in a mocking dip. "If you're sure . . ." he wasn't talking about fixing the door, and he knew she knew it.

"I'm sure," she said softly.

He stared at her for another long moment and then without saying goodbye, he went out, going through a door that now opened and closed very silently.

6

The following week a merciless Dakota winter settled in. The frigid wind, blowing directly from Canada, poured unimpeded over the bleak prairie. Crusted, glittering snow collapsed under Raine's feet as she walked back and forth between Julia's house and the print shop. She hardly noticed the weather. An even colder chill was settled around her heart. She moved through her days in a numbed state, holding at bay thoughts of Jade and Michele together. She worked on the paper and talked to Julia as if nothing had happened—but something had. A very deep and private part of her, unable to stand the pain, had gone into hiding.

Her only consolation was Tate. She had made arrangements to take him sledding on their next Saturday together, and knowing she would be seeing him again was the only thing that made the week tolerable. But when Saturday morning came and Jade brought Tate into Julia's little house, she ignored the sudden thrust of agony at seeing Jade again and stared at Tate. His small face was downcast, his mouth turned down, and he looked everywhere but at Raine.

The glossy material of her ski coat whispered as she squatted to bring his face on eye level with hers. She lifted his small, pointed chin up with her finger. "Hey, sport. Why so unhappy?"

He only stared at her with those large, dark eyes. Disturbed, she lifted her head to Jade. "What's wrong?"

"He didn't want to come today," Jade said in a bland tone.

She straightened, a cold chill feathering down her spine, her hand lingering on Tate's shoulder. "Why not?"

"Actually," Jade thrust his hand into the pocket of his jeans, pushing back the corner of his open sheepskin jacket, "it's your fault."

Her eyes darkened. "What did I do?"

"You took him to see Tom Cannon's puppies." Jade shrugged. "We went back Tuesday night and brought one home." He glanced down at his small son's up-turned face. "Tate didn't want to leave the dog."

Raine's face tightened. "Why didn't you call me? We could have put off the sledding expedition until next week."

Jade stood and looked at her, his eyes probing, his mouth drawn up in a cynical smile. He didn't say anything, but his eyes spoke volumes. *You wouldn't have believed me.*

A hard jolt shook her. His acceptance of her mistrust rocked her to the core. It was wrong, somehow.

Shaking inside, more disturbed than she dared show, she thrust the thought to the back of her mind and stooped down again to look into Tate's face. "Honey, I don't blame you for not wanting to leave your new friend home alone. Let's go and get your dog and take him along with us, shall we?"

Tate's face brightened with a blazing smile. "Can we?"

"Of course. He'll have fun out in the snow, too."

Tate sparkled with happiness. "I wanted to bring him. But Daddy said you might not like having to watch out for a dog as well as a boy."

To be fair, she supposed Jade was right in being

cautious about foisting a strange animal on her along with his son. "I think I can handle it."

Tate shot a triumphant glance at his father. "See, Daddy? She says she can handle it," he parroted, obviously enjoying his childish version of I-told-you-so.

"Your Aunt Raine has courage," he murmured.

Her name in his smoky voice rippled down her spine. She fought against her instinctive reaction.

"But since you're going to take the dog," he went on, "I think I'll go along to lend an extra hand."

She hadn't expected that. She straightened and met his eyes. "That isn't necessary. Doug is meeting us out there." Disturbed, far more susceptible to him than she had thought she would be, she said the words bluntly and stood waiting for him to withdraw his offer to go with her.

His face kept its smooth, expressionless look. "If you've made arrangements with Martin, I'll take Tate home. He can go sledding another day."

Her cheeks burned. That was a low blow, and he knew it. Tate's protest came immediately. "Daddy, no. I don't want to go home. I want to go with Aunt Raine."

She saw the quicksilver gleam of satisfaction in Jade's eyes and was angrier than ever. He had used Tate and neatly boxed her in. The slight, mocking smile on his lips told her he had done it purposely. For what reason? "If we stand here arguing all day, we'll never get any sledding done. Why don't you and your dad go home and get the puppy and meet us out at Willow Hill?"

"Will you, Daddy? Will you please?"

"If that's what your Aunt Raine wants . . ." The words were silky, lazy. She fought down the pounding of anger at her throat and said, "Tate can go back with you and hold the dog. I'll meet you there."

"Why don't you ride along?" Jade countered, tightening the net and watching her while he did it, his lips curved in that disturbingly mocking smile. "There's no reason to take two cars."

"Ride with us, Aunt Raine, please." Tate jumped up and down, his boots clumping on the polished wood of Julia's entryway.

Knowing full well that Jade had maneuvered her once again into an untenable position, she thought about giving him a curt "no"—and knew she couldn't do it. Tate was sensitive to rejection since Michele had gone and he wouldn't understand. She gave in, and regretted it the minute she climbed into the pickup. Jade lifted Tate onto the middle of the seat, but he immediately begged to sit by the window. If she refused, Jade would guess the reason. She steeled herself, smiled at Tate, and let him squeeze by her knees to the other side of her. Wriggling like the puppy they were going home to get, the boy bounced up and down on the seat and looked out the window at the frosty landscape. Every bounce seemed to force her a little closer to Jade.

Jade hadn't bothered to fasten his jacket and it rasped over his denim pants as he turned the wheel and drove away from the house. His hands were bare, strong and brown with a shadowing of his tan from last summer under the light golden hairs. Fur-lined gloves protruded from his pocket and brushed the side of her hip. Even in her warm outdoor clothing, she was so overwhelmingly aware of him that her skin burned.

She turned her head and looked out the window, away from him. The winter sun shimmered off the snow and spangled it with a sequin brightness that made her blink. They drove along Jade's land and a calf broke away from the rest of the herd and nosed through the gray rail fence to give them a large, brown-eyed stare. His coat was a thick red, a rusty contrast to the white snow. The sky was a typical South Dakota sky, a stretch of vivid blue that had no beginning or end.

"Beautiful morning," Jade murmured softly.

"Yes. Yes, it is."

"Are you warm enough?"

Afraid to trust her voice the second time, she nodded.

"Are we keeping Martin waiting?"

She shook her head. "He had something to do first. He planned to join us a little bit later, around eleven."

"That's good," Jade murmured. "I wouldn't want to make him wait for you out in the cold."

Angered, she said coolly, "I'm sure he won't mind."

Jade's mouth tightened and he said nothing more for the rest of the trip. At the ranch, she stayed in the pickup while Jade and Tate went inside and got the dog, a collie puppy. A fluff of sable and white, the dog squirmed in Tate's arms. A thump at the rear of the truck told her that Jade had thrown an extra sled in the back. He came round and climbed in under the wheel beside her, and now there were two wriggling bodies to push her closer to Jade instead of one. The puppy leaped and struggled to get a better aim at Tate's face and lavish him with pink-tongued kisses. Tate closed his eyes and squealed, loving every minute of it.

Willow Hill was a long, sloping mound of land that rose out of the prairie and swept down to a narrow riverlet of water gurgling over a stony bed. The hill took its name from the fountain-shaped willows whose roots drank the water from underneath the creek bed. Green, arching branches shaded the winding stream in the summertime but now the willows were barren tangled masses of snakelike branches. The town of Verylon had long ago bought the land from the harried farmer who grew weary of trying to keep people away from the only hill for miles around.

Jade pulled the pickup into an improvised parking area at the top of the hill. Tate was out in a flash, but before he could bound away to the crest of the hill, Raine scrambled out of the pickup and snatched him inelegantly by the seat of his snowsuit. "Not so fast, sport. You know the rules."

Tate protested with an indignant, affronted-male look in his eyes that reminded Raine strongly of Jade. "Let me go."

"Everybody takes his own sled," Raine said implacably.

Tate stared up at her for a moment warily, as if he were studying her to see if she meant what she said. "I have to watch my puppy."

Tate's "sled" was a bright blue plastic dish with a rope attached. Jade looped the rope over his son's shoulder and Raine knew that would be the end of Tate's protest. Tate cast a rueful look at his father, hitched the rope to a more secure place on his shoulder in adult acceptance of his burden and turned his eyes back to Raine. "Now can I go?"

Raine looked at him. "Wait for us at the top of the hill."

Tate hurried away, his boots clomping over the snow, his dish sled bumping behind him, the puppy scrambling alongside. And suddenly, in that brilliant, frigid cold that already had her cheeks tingling, she was left alone with Jade.

He had gotten the sleds out of the pickup and he turned and put a rope in her mittened hand. "Everybody takes his own sled," he murmured, his mouth tilting.

She took it, glad that her ski jacket and gloves prevented her from feeling the brush of his hand. "Do you object to my teaching your son responsibility?"

"Not at all," he murmured. "I'm just . . . surprised."

"Why?" She turned away from him and began to walk toward the hill where Tate danced around the puppy as the dog made rushing dives at his boots.

"I would think you'd indulge him in order to assure his continuing devotion."

"I don't have to do that," she shot back, annoyed. "Tate's too young and too honest to put a price tag on his affection."

"Is he?" Jade murmured.

Raine's eyes flashed. "He couldn't be bought . . . any more than you could."

"Nice to know you think so highly of me."

"I didn't say I think highly of you. I said you couldn't be bought."

"I'll spare you the obvious answer to that." His smile mocked her.

She shook her head. "Which is?"

"Everyone can be bought, if the price is right."

The chill breeze lifted the strands of her long gold-brown hair, feathering them over the silky material of her ski jacket. "That's not true."

He grasped her arm, dragging her closer to him, bringing his face down close to hers. "My God, I wish I could live in that rose-colored world you inhabit."

A long streamer of her hair fanned across her face and caught in her lips. Before she could brush it away, his hand was there, gliding over her cheek, pushing the lock of hair gently to one side. She stood silently, feeling those calloused fingertips against her mouth, aching to kiss that work-hardened male hand, and hating herself for it. "And I couldn't live in your colorless world, Jade."

He dropped his hand and her skin cooled. "So you're consigning me to hell."

The words came out with a flat, dead sound. She battered down the quick, empathetic ache. "You've made your own purgatory. I had nothing to do with it."

"Didn't you?"

A whole world opened up before her with those two words, a world she had glimpsed once but knew she would never enter. She couldn't listen to those words, couldn't accept the enticing thought that what she did or thought made a difference to Jade. He was simply playing with her. After being with Michele, he was no doubt forced to recognize that his body had physical needs. And he wanted her to satisfy them.

Under her winter clothing, her body burned. Anger was her only defense. "What's the matter? Did you suddenly remember that Michele is two thousand miles away and I'm here, right at hand?" The words were harsh, raw-edged. "Are you thinking you made the wrong choice?"

He grasped her arm, his eyes flashing. "I made the wrong choice long ago. . . ."

"Daddy, are you coming? My puppy wants to go for a ride with me."

For a moment longer, his eyes impaled her. Then he tore them away and let go of her to gaze down at Tate. The boy was fidgeting with impatience and the dog, sensitive to his young master's mood, danced and skittered on the snow at his feet.

"We're coming," she soothed him, turning away from Jade, trying to take a deep breath of the frosty air.

She gathered Tate's mittened hand in hers and walked away with him, listening to his chatter with half of her concentration, thinking she'd been a fool to come. Why hadn't she simply bowed out of the trip when Jade insisted on coming along?

You came because you wanted to be with him. You've always wanted to be with him.

Tightening the belt of her ski jacket, she looked down at Tate. "Get in and I'll give you a start."

Tate climbed in eagerly. She gave him a vigorous push that sent the saucer skittering over the snow and down the hill.

Tensed, waiting, she shaded her eyes against the white brilliance and watched as Tate clung to the turning, twisting circle of bright blue plastic and managed to stay upright.

"Do you want the toboggan?"

Brown and glossy with varnish, it was a short one, meant for three people. Surely she could handle it alone. "Yes."

He gave her the rope and she sat down on the cold wood, tucking her feet under the protective curve. "I'm ready."

The snow crunched under his boots. She braced herself, waiting for the jolt that would tell her he had pushed her into motion. Instead, he sat down behind her, wrapping her in the hard strength of his legs. The sudden warmth of his body shielding hers from the wind was comforting—and soul-destroying. Before she could utter a protest, he snugged her into the curve of his body and wrapped his arms around her waist. "Ready?"

"No. Jade . . ."

He pushed off with his feet, sending the toboggan over the crest. The wind blew her words out of her mouth, tousled the long length of her hair under her knit cap and feathered it back over Jade. If it was in his face, he made no move to brush it away. He merely tightened his grip and created a wonderful shelter for her. They sailed over a hard bump, bounced, and picked up speed. The wind and the cold and the speed were exhilarating, as wildly exciting as the feel of Jade's arms around her and the rub of her hips against the curve of his body. Down and down they flew, picking up momentum as the earth fell away in front of them. In one last spurt of speed, the toboggan slid to a curving stop at the bottom of the hill. Thrown forward and then back, Raine felt the hard muscles of his arms gripping her in a protective hold. Then all motion ceased.

Jade didn't get up. He sat holding her in that intimate position. Her heart thundered and, sure that he could hear it, her mind issued the command to move. Her muscles refused, while her nerves sent the heady message of Jade's proximity straight to her brain and she savored every moment of his nearness.

"All right?" he said softly.

Brought back to reality with a jolt, she said, "Yes, of course."

Another minute of time passed. He moved, slowly straightening up. His boots planted firmly in the snow, he held out his hand. She took it, feeling the fine balance of his body as he braced himself to take the weight of hers.

He pulled her up . . . too hard, too fast. She slammed into him, and felt the rock-hard readiness of his muscles waiting to receive her weight. He had done it on purpose. Instantly, his arms encircled her and just as instantly, her body sang into life.

Determined not to let him know how much he disturbed her, she pushed her hands against his chest. "Thanks for the help." Her tone was dry and ironic. His hands tightened. "Anytime."

She stood in his arms, unwilling to struggle, afraid to reveal her eagerness to be away from him. He held her for another long, tantalizing moment. Then his hands slid slowly down her arms and left her. A chill racked her that had nothing to do with cold. Free of his grip, she turned away, determined not to betray her reaction to his nearness and vowing to stay off that sled. But the next minute, Tate was beside them, begging to be taken on the toboggan. Jade, squinting against the sun on the snow, his mouth tilted in that mocking male challenge, insisted that she ride along.

She was caught. If she refused, he would know that his nearness disturbed her. If she went, she would be forced to let him touch her, hold her. Refusing to examine the truth too closely, she went.

Again and again, Jade tucked his son in the front, helped her settle in the middle, enfolded her in his embrace and pushed off. Again and again, she gritted her teeth and steeled herself against the feel of his chest against her back, his hard thighs clamped around her hips, his arms around her waist. It was a contest of wills, a battle she must win.

Supremely unaware of the tension between the two adults he loved, Tate enjoyed every minute of the exciting rides. He laughed, a high-pitched cry of glee as they flew with daredevil speed over the snow. The puppy yipped in furious reply and scrambled down the hill beside them, struggling to keep upright on the slippery snow.

On the third trip, the dog ran in front of the toboggan

and nearly met an untimely end. Tate became frightened by his pet's near-miss with danger and insisted on holding the dog in his lap for the next trip down the hill.

Raine said quickly, "You go ahead without me." Jade raked her with an amused, mocking smile. Deliberately, she cast an anxious look in the direction of the road. "I'll stay here and wait for Doug."

A sudden frown, a tightening of the amber gold brows drew grooves above the bridge of his nose. "All right. We'll go ahead without you." He sat down behind Tate and the dog and with one powerful thrust of his leg sent them down over the crest of the hill, the tall dark figure protectively hugging the small boy. Jade loved Tate just as he had loved Tate's mother. Would Jade ever get over loving her beautiful sister and feeling bitterly hurt? She didn't know. Jade wasn't a man to reveal his feelings but that didn't mean he didn't have any. He'd asked her to come to him that day of the wedding. What if she'd gone? What if she'd given herself to him freely, without restraint as she had always wanted to do? Suppose they had made love. Would he have found the strength to cancel his trip to New York and stay away from Michele?

A bitter taste rose in her throat. Being the object of his physical desire wasn't enough. She wanted more, so much more. And Jade had nothing to give.

There was nothing left for her to do but keep busy with her work at the print shop and sublimate her love for Jade by spending her weekends with his son. At this moment, a life devoid of Jade seemed as bleak as the snowy field in front of her. How long could she go on pretending indifference to that lean male body that had settled in behind her on every run? How long could she ignore the sensations that bombarded her when Jade touched her? How long could she deny her own reaction to his eyes moving over her? Each time he had sat down on the sled behind her, she had become more addicted to the feel of those muscled legs and that lithe male form under his open jacket. Her resolve to stay away from him had weakened with every trip down that hill. His body was that of a cowboy, broad shouldered and narrow-waisted with a flat, hard-muscled stomach that gravity would never pull into a paunch. How long could she go on before she gave in to Jade—and to her own desperate longing to know his body in the most intimate way of all?

She blocked that agonizing thought out of her mind and turned to stare at the road. Doug's blue Volkswagen was nowhere in sight. Had she misunderstood him? She didn't think so. Where was he?

A half-hour later, thoroughly chilled from standing around, she accepted the fact that Doug wasn't coming. For some reason, he hadn't been able to keep their date, and of course he had no way of letting her know. She stomped her feet on the hard-packed snow and stuffed her mittened hands into her pockets. Cold penetrated into her bones. Even dressed as warmly as she was, her inactivity allowed too much body heat to escape.

Jade had not invited her to ride on the sled again, but when he saw her moving in a restless attempt to get warm, he said, "Sure you wouldn't like one more ride?"

Whatever it cost him to ask, it cost her more to refuse. "No thanks, I'm fine."

He didn't move away immediately, and she felt his eyes going over her, even though she was looking away from him, out over the road. After a long, vibrant moment, he turned away and sat down on the sled with Tate. They flew over the crest of the hill, but when they trudged back up afterward, Jade said to Tate, "I think that's enough for today, son. Your Aunt Raine is turning blue."

Tate squinted up at her and said very practically, "Where? I don't see any blue spots."

"They're not in places where you can see them," his father drawled, his eyes dropping to her chest.

"Please don't change your plans on my account. I'm

fine." She hugged her arms around her and made a half-turn away from Jade to gaze beyond his shoulder at the road.

"Still think he's coming?" Jade's voice was quiet.

She shook her head. "Something's happened. He may have gotten a call from his boss. He often does on Saturdays."

"Tough luck," Jade said unsympathetically.

"We're not all lucky enough to work for ourselves," she retorted, her voice as crisp and cool as the air around her.

Tate, holding the puppy, squinted up at her. "You sound just like Mommy used to before she left. Are you going to get mad and go away, too?"

Over the top of Tate's head, her eyes met Jade's, and for one blinding moment, a fierce blaze of emotion flared in those green depths, an emotion so powerful she could feel it to the tips of her frozen toes. Shaken, she stooped down to Tate and caught his shoulder with a mittened hand. "Of course not, honey. I'm not going anywhere no matter how mad I sound." She took off her mitten and brushed his snow-wet cheek with her hand, wishing she could brush away his apprehensions along with the dampness and smiled at the boy, forcing brightness into her tone. "I've got a paper to get out every week, remember?"

"I remember," Tate said solemnly.

Abruptly, Jade swiveled away. Upset that Tate thought her as capable of deserting him as Michele had been, she watched as Jade collected the toboggan and the dish sled and lifted them both into the back of the truck.

Moments later, they were on their way. Beside her on the seat, Tate was quiet. Even the puppy seemed subdued. She felt exhausted herself, though she'd done only half the hill climbing Jade and Tate had, and it was barely past noon. She closed her eyes against the glare of the sun and shut out her thoughts as well.

The heater didn't begin to take the chill away. It did warm her a little though, but when they came to a stop and she opened her eyes, a chill that had nothing to do with cold flared through her. They were in the yard in front of Jade's house.

"Why didn't you take me back to town?"

"Tate and I decided you should stay for lunch."

"I can't do that . . ."

"You can't do anything else unless you feel like walking five miles back to town."

She didn't feel like walking at all, and five miles back to town was out of the question. Of course, she could have lunch with Tate and Jade. Tate would be an adequate chaperone. Not that she thought she needed to be protected from Jade. It was her own errant thoughts that spelled danger, and surely, in Tate's presence, she could control those.

She hadn't been in the house in ages, but once she walked inside, she felt as if she had never been away. She remembered how the light streamed down through the skylight in the open entryway and how the contemporary house, built of glass and cedar, had always made her feel so comfortable and at home with its open-beamed ceiling and feeling of light and space. The house had been the topic of conversation for almost a year after it was finished. The people in Verylon were skeptical about its ability to stand up against the severe weather. Harry had told him one good prairie wind would blow the whole thing away. "That peaked roof will catch every breeze," he'd told Jade bluntly. "With all that glass, you'll freeze to death in the wintertime. Cost you a fortune to heat it."

But Jade had gone over the plans with the architect carefully, searching for flaws in the house. There were none. Now, nestled in the trees Jade had planted seven years ago, the house was as beautiful as it had been the day it was completed. And strangely enough, she thought, as she walked into the living room with its plush leather couch built into the sunken conversation pit around the fireplace, it wasn't Michele she remembered as she looked around. It was the ghost of herself, cleaning, rearranging furniture, picking up Michele's magazines that she had strewn on the floor, vacuuming the bronze carpeting.

"Here, let me take your coat," Jade said, after he had instructed Tate to sit down on the floor and unzip his boots.

His fingers grazed hers and she couldn't control the shiver that racked her body. His eyes, darkly concerned, probed her face. "Are you that cold?"

"No . . ." He hung up her coat and unceremoniously clasped her hand, breathing in sharply when her cold flesh came in contact with his warm palm. "My God, woman, your hands are like icebergs." He shrugged out of his coat and stowed it away. "Go on upstairs to the bathroom and run a tub of hot water."

Sitting at Jade's feet, Tate had removed one boot. Now he worked on the other, his tongue caught between his teeth at the side of his mouth. In spite of Tate's presence, her mind served up another occasion when he had suggested she take a hot bath. She turned away to look around the house as if she were a polite guest. "I'm fine," she said, folding her arms around her midriff in a vain attempt to warm her hands.

Moving behind her, shielding her from Tate, he said in a low, lethal undertone directly into her ear, "Do you think you're safe because Tate is here? Believe me, you're not." He paused, his breath moving her hair. "If what you really want is for me to carry you up there and strip you myself, I'd be more than happy to oblige." From behind her, his hand started at her elbow and slid along her clasped arms until his fingertips grazed the peak of her breast.

"Take your hands off of me," she ordered in a husky undertone as quiet as his.

"Only if you go up those stairs and take a bath," he murmured, the words softly menacing, "or are you resisting because you like my method of persuasion?"

"Your 'method of persuasion' doesn't . . . affect me in the slightest," she got out between gritted teeth.

"Stay here," he murmured, "and I'll expand on the theme." Above her cradled arms, the arrogantly male fingers brushed over her breasts in a slow, circular path. Even through the heavy wool of her sweater, the caress was heady, devastating. She fought to contain the leap of nerves under her skin and to stand rock still under his insolent handling.

"Would you really like me to prove you aren't as immune to my touch as you'd like me to believe?" Lightly, deftly, his fingertips grazed her. There was no way she could deny the evidence of her arousal. Her own body betrayed her.

"Stop touching me," she ordered in a gritty undertone.

"Are you going to go up and take a bath?" His fingers possessed her even more intimately, claiming the hard bud that bloomed to his touch. His lips found a soft, vulnerable place behind her ear.

A warmth flared upward from the pit of her stomach. Oh, dear God, even like this, with Jade touching her just to prove his power over her, she still wanted him. With a low cry, she wrenched away and ran to the stairs. As she bounded up the half flight, his soft laughter trailed after her, along with Tate's childish voice saying, "What's the matter with Aunt Raine, Daddy?"

What Jade's answer was, she didn't know. She didn't want to know. She didn't want to think about how even that cavalier exploration of her breast through her sweater had made her want to turn in his arms and let him touch her in any way he wanted to.

She walked down the hall past his bedroom and into the main bathroom, her body alive with sensual need. She closed and locked the door and stripped off her clothes. Naked, she went through the cupboard, found some bubble liquid Jade obviously kept for Tate, and tipped the container over the running water. She reached back in the cupboard to bring out two dark brown fluffy towels that were the exact shade of the fixtures and wrapped one around her head. She left the other lying on the countertop of the vanity.

She slid into the warm water. It closed around her like a caress and, once again, she was reminded that she was a woman and that she had felt the touch of a man. Stifling the urge to climb back out and take a cold shower instead, she stayed where she was, knowing that her body needed the warmth of the water after being out in the cold.

She leaned back and sank into the water to her shoulders. For several moments, she luxuriated in the warmth. Time hung suspended. She didn't try to think. She didn't try to do anything but feel the wonderful, tingling warmth seeping into her toes, her feet, her legs. Unbidden, a vision of Jade drifted into her mind, Jade, sitting with his legs around her as he had on the sled—but gloriously naked this time, lounging in the bathtub behind her, sliding her into the hollow of his body just as he had a dozen times that morning, with nothing between them but silky water.

A heated hunger rose from a deep feminine center—a hunger that could never be satisfied. She climbed out of the tub, snatched up the brown towel, and rubbed herself briskly. But she couldn't rub away the memory of Jade's experienced, knowing fingers playing over the sensitive tips of her breasts.

She snatched up her clothes. Her jeans and heavy sweater felt several degrees cooler than her body, but she got into them, knowing she had no other choice. Clothed, she felt calmer. Convinced that she was in control, she combed her hair and stepped out into the hall—only to slam head on into Jade's broad chest.

He dropped Tate's hand and caught her arms to steady

her. "Easy," he said softly, but the word had the exact opposite effect on her. Disturbed by the sudden, hot memory of her bathtub fantasy, she shuddered and twisted away from him.

He frowned and let her go.

"Daddy, what's the matter?"

He looked down at his son. Tate returned his gaze owlishly. Jade said, "Nothing. I was just catching your Aunt Raine so she won't fall down." His eyes swung back to Raine and those green depths mocked.

Raine struggled for composure and glanced at Tate. "Are you going in for a nap, sport?"

Tate nodded. "Daddy said if I slept now, he'd let me go out to the barn later and play with my puppy."

She stooped down and brushed his cheek with her lips. "That sounds like a good idea. You have a good sleep."

From over her head, Jade said, "I'll tuck him in and be down to fix your lunch in a few minutes."

Each slow word mocked her lack of composure. She rose to her feet and met his eyes. "Take your time. I can fix my own."

"Fine. Be my guest." His words lingered in her ears as he turned and went on down the hall with his small son in tow.

Her face burning, she walked down the stairs, only too aware that they would be eating together without the buffering presence of Tate.

She had prepared many meals in Jade's modern kitchen and the light, bright room done in yellow and white was as airy and clean as it had been then. On the round table in the eating area of the room sat the remains of Tate's lunch, a half of a peanut butter and jelly sandwich along with a quarter of a glass of milk. Jade had cut and pared an apple, but Tate had barely touched it.

Automatically, she opened the refrigerator and surveyed the contents. There were plenty of eggs and an added bonus, a half-dozen red peppers. After she had chopped the peppers and set them to sauté in butter, she took out five eggs, broke them into a bowl and began to whip them vigorously, venting some of her anger. Outside the window, the snowy landscape glittered like a sea of diamonds. It was flat land that held no barriers for the eye, and it all belonged to Jade. He'd acquired yet another section since Michele left. There seemed to be no limit to the amount of range land he could absorb into his operation. He was expert at everything. She turned away from the window and went to the stove to pour the eggs over the browning peppers, remembering the spring she had stayed there with Michele. Weary of housework, she'd gone out and ridden the range with the men, helping to bring in the newborn calves from the range. She'd watched Jade, bare to the waist in the freaky sudden heat of that April, go into the temporary corral they'd rigged for the calves and mothers and snag the calf he wanted with one clean throw of his rope. She remembered the way his muscles moved under the skin of his back, and the way the perspiration made his skin gleam. She'd gone into the house after that and stayed there, safely away from the sight of him.

The omelet simmered in the pan. Restlessly, she turned back to the window again. In the distance, the cattle clustered around the long outdoor troughs, eating the hay Jade had harvested last summer from three hundred acres of land. A partially completed lean-to protected the cattle from the north wind. Jade had begun to build cattle sheds scattered in strategic places over his ranch, but the winter weather had put a stop to his building projects. In another two months, he'd be back at work, or sooner, if the weather broke. It had been a hard winter. It had been cold and they'd had several snow storms, but none had been a full-blown blizzard like the twenty-inch snow storm they had gotten the winter before Tate was born.

"Something smells good." Jade's low voice came from behind her. She turned. He stood watching her with those dark green eyes, leaning against the edge of the table, lazily at ease.

She strove to dampen her reaction to his sudden presence and braced herself to sound cool and impersonal. "It's an omelet. I'm just ready to dish it out. How about setting the table?"

"My pleasure."

After he had set out the plates and flatware, he made a pot of coffee and they sat down to eat in a companionable silence.

A few minutes later, Jade pushed his plate away. "That was delicious. Thank you."

"You're welcome."

"You cooked, I'll clean up. You go into the living room and relax."

"No, I . . . think I'd better go home. I . . . I have things to do."

He gazed at her. "Are you afraid you'll miss Martin's call?"

"No, of course not."

"Then go sit down. I'll take care of things here." The words were cool and commanding.

She hesitated, her protest hovering on her lips. Yet he was only asking her to wait a few more moments. Surely she could do that. "All right." She turned and walked out of the room, anxious to escape those lazily examining eyes.

A few minutes later, Jade came into the living room. "I thought I told you to sit down and relax." She was in the raised part of the living room, standing in front of the glass wall. She had been looking out over the ranch buildings, but at the sound of Jade's voice, she turned. "Are you ready to take me back?"

"I can't go and leave Tate alone in the house."

"Of course, how stupid of me. I'll call Julia and . . ."

He took a step closer. "Are you running away from me because I touched you?"

She stood in the sunlight that streamed in from the

window and met his eyes, her own clear and expressive. "No."

He grimaced as if she had struck him. "I wouldn't have . . . if I hadn't been damn sick and tired of seeing you stand and freeze to death on the top of the hill because you were watching for your lover."

Her chin came up. "Why should that bother you?"

He took another step. "Why do you think?"

"You can't be . . . jealous."

"Why not?"

"Jealousy implies caring."

At this he was silent. She knew he couldn't deny her words, and the thought twisted inside her like a knife.

He read the look on her face and made a despairing gesture with his hand. "What do you want from me? Empty words? *I love you, Raine.* Is that what you want to hear?".

Yes. Yes. Oh, dear God, yes! But not in that bitter, acid tone.

He shook his head, his eyes gleaming with desire. "We don't need love," he said in a soft, intent tone.

Her shoulders sagged and she turned away to look out the window again. "If you wait long enough, Michele will be back." She shook her head. "I can't be your . . . amusement in the meantime."

"If she does come back, I wouldn't let her in the house," he said coldly.

"You can't mean that."

"I do mean it. If you have some thought of staying away from me because of Michele, forget it."

"It's not because of Michele that I . . ." she kept her back to him. She didn't dare face him. She had the feeling that she was melting, that the sound of his voice was wiping everything out of her eyes and heart but her love for him.

"Then why do you push me away?"

He had moved closer. The soft tone came from directly behind her. She stared out over the ranch, seeing the buildings that clustered around the house—the machine shed, the bunkhouse that would soon be filled with the men Jade hired as temporary help, the barn, the silos. His farm complex was neat and compact, well-organized and efficient, like the owner.

The slight brush of his chest on her back warned her that he was directly behind her, but the warning hadn't come soon enough. She was trapped between his body and the glass window. Before she could twist away, he locked her to him, his arms circled in front of her. She stood in shocked silence, fighting the pleasure of being pulled back against his chest until their bodies touched from shoulder to thigh. When she did not move in protest, his right hand slid lower and his fingers splayed over her abdomen. The feel of his palm, even over her denims, sent a tingle of erotic pleasure coursing through her body. His other hand glided under her sweater and began pushing it upward in an agonizingly slow path from navel to waist to rib cage. At last he found the treasure he sought, and when he cupped and supported her warm flesh, the contrast between the coolness of the air and the heat of his touch made her gasp. He laughed softly, a sound of masculine amusement, and nuzzled her hair aside to nibble at the soft skin of her neck even while his hand on her abdomen began to make slow, sensuous circles.

"Jade, no . . ." It was a token protest, one only her mouth made, unaccompanied by any attempt to push herself away, and he knew it.

"Shh," he said softly. "Relax, Raine. Take the pleasure I can give you." His mouth wandered deeper under the tunnel of her hair and his tongue flicked against a tiny, ultrasensitive spot at her nape, just above her backbone. He homed in on it with the precision of a marksman. The intimate touch of his warm tongue sent raking shudders through her. His hand cupping the underside of her breast registered the shiver. "I wanted to hold you like this all morning. Every time I sat down behind you on that sled, I kept thinking of the softness of your breasts and the pleasure I feel when I touch you. And I'm not the only one who enjoys it, am I? I can feel you absorbing my caresses as if you've been craving them for a long time. Are you as hungry for me as I am for you?"

She didn't answer. She knew she should push him away, but she wanted his hands to continue that slow, circular teasing at the junction of her thighs until he took her to the ragged edge of a precipice from which there was no turning back.

"Come upstairs with me, Raine."

She wanted to. Oh, she wanted to. But he didn't love her. And he didn't want her love. She could take what he had to give, and pretend, just for a little while, that he was hers. But when it was over, he would know the depth of her love. She wouldn't be able to hide her feelings behind curt words. He would know that she loved him, and he would pity her. Out of that pity, he might feel compelled to marry her. The thought stung. She shook her head.

Roughly, he turned her in his arms, his hands holding the sweater away from her bare flesh. The violence in his eyes might have frightened her if he had been any other man, but the glitter in Jade's aroused an excited fever inside her that nearly overrode her reason. Her head high, she made no move to cover herself.

A muscle moved on the side of his jaw, and abruptly, he dropped his hands from her arms, letting the sweater fall. "I've let you go more times than I want to think about," he said in a softly insolent tone, his eyes moving down to the feminine curves that were now covered, the mocking glitter reminding her that he had seen her bare flesh on more than one occasion, and that today she had done nothing to protect herself from his gaze.

She met his eyes with her chin high. In that same, soft tone he warned, "But don't think I'll ever do it again. Now go call Julia."

7

Toward the end of March, when the streets were slushy with melting snow, and Raine finally began to sleep a little better, Patty Harson came into the print shop, carrying a piece of paper. "I've written this," she said anxiously, thrusting it toward Raine. "Would you print it in next week's paper?"

Julia was running the press. She looked up curiously, but didn't move. The press had to be watched so that it didn't double over paper or tear it indiscriminately. Raine glanced over the note, then raised her eyes back to Patty. "I hadn't heard a word about this. They're thinking of closing the school?"

Patty nodded.

Raine shook her head. "I can't run this unless I know for sure that it isn't a rumor."

"Call Stephen Clark. He's the president of the school board. If you don't get a straight answer from him—"

"I'll do that."

"If you decide not to print it, call me, will you?"

"I will." Patty went out, and Raine reached for the phone. Stephen was out in the field, his wife said. After several tries, Raine did finally speak with him, but his answers were evasive. She cradled the phone and read

116

Patty's article over again. It was a simple, straightforward plea for the truth. Patty suggested that the school board talk openly to the community and let them know whether there was any truth to the rumor that Verylon was in danger of losing its school. Raine laid the sheet on the desk and sat back. She thought of the article she had printed last fall about the cheerleaders. She remembered the pride on their faces and their eager enthusiasm for their school teams. Her decision made, she stood up, carried the article over to her machine and began to set it in type.

The article generated a lot of discussion, but not much action from the school board. They still hid behind evasive answers and conciliatory statements. Raine offered each of them equal space in print, but none of the board availed themselves of the privilege.

Throughout the spring, rumors flew. Toward the end of May, when the school year was finished, the truth came out. Verylon was, indeed, going to lose its school. After the coming school year was over, the children would be bussed into Canton and absorbed in the school system there. There was rage and dismay and loud protests, but there was nothing that could be done. It was a blow to the town, and to the *Verylon Appeal* newspaper.

Toward the last of June, on a particularly hot day, Doug sat on the corner of Raine's desk and swung one leg. His summer shirt was open at the throat, and he looked cool and comfortable, even though the air was heavy and hot inside the print shop. She sat in the swivel chair behind the desk, feeling the perspiration drip down her back and wishing she were home in a cool shower. Doug was well launched into one of his many stories and he showed no signs of stopping. He was telling her about a newspaper office his dad had supplied when he first started out in the business in the Pacific Northwest. "They had a lady Linotype operator named Mabel

Johnson. Everybody called her Johnny. Anyway, the roof leaked right over Johnny's Linotype machine. She asked the boss to fix it repeatedly and he ignored her. One morning after a hard rain, she found a puddle of water under her swivel chair. She stomped out into the back room, came back with a push broom and pushed the water all the way up to the nice new carpeting the boss had just had laid around his front desk." Doug grinned. "The repairmen were there to fix the roof the next morning."

Raine smiled. "Who says women were subservient in the good old days?"

"Not me. My grandfather's sister homesteaded here in South Dakota."

Raine's interest was piqued. "Alone?"

"You mean without a husband? You bet. My grandfather was on the neighboring one hundred and sixty, so he was close by, but he wasn't much help. He had his own problems."

"Did she . . . stay long enough to claim the land?"

Doug shook his head. "But it wasn't the cold or the loneliness that drove her out. She was over in the dry part of Dakota, next to the Black Hills, and she didn't have a source of water and couldn't get a well."

"How long did she stay?"

"She was there one summer and one winter I think Dad said."

"She must have been made of tough stuff."

Doug grinned. "I come from good prairie stock. Speaking of which," he slid off the desk, "if I can't talk you into ordering more *paper* stock, I'd better be on my way to someplace where people appreciate my company's products."

"I'm sorry I can't order more, Doug. Everything's on hold in this town right now. Our advertising has dropped off and so has our subscription list. We're going to lose our school and Matt says he's going to close the grocery store next fall." She tipped her head and looked up at him. "And if he does that," she shrugged and tried to look philosophical, "we'll lose our biggest source of ad revenue. The paper will fold. We can't survive in a town that's drying up."

Doug looked startled. "When did all this come about?"

"Talk's been going around town since last winter, but I haven't said anything, because I thought that's all it was—talk. But now we know it isn't."

"If the paper folds, what will you do?"

"Drive to Canton and look for a job, I guess."

"You wouldn't leave?"

"Where would I go? Besides, I can't leave Julia . . . or Tate."

"You really love that little guy, don't you?" He watched her, his face sobering as she nodded. He gazed at her for a moment more and then picked up his satchel. "Look, if there's anything I can do—"

"If you hear of a job opening anywhere around you might let me know," she said wryly.

He nodded. "Will do."

He was at the door when she remembered. "Doug." Her voice stopped him as he was reaching for the door. "Yes?"

"The Commercial Club is having a Fourth of July picnic here in the town park to try to bolster people's interest and pride in Verylon. Would you like to come as my guest?"

She'd thought about asking him for a long time, almost a month. The Fourth of July picnic was the first time she would be seeing Jade for a prolonged period of time and she needed Doug as a buffer. She knew it wasn't fair to him, but . . .

He rubbed his chin thoughtfully with his free hand. "Does that mean you're going to provide the food?"

She laughed. "No, it means the Commercial Club is going to provide the food. I'm buying your ticket."

"Sounds like an offer too good to refuse. What time?"

"How does eleven sound? Dinner will be served around twelve, of course."

Doug rolled his eyes. "Of course. The people of South Dakota expire if they don't eat at noon."

"There are races and games in the afternoon and fireworks at night."

Doug grinned. "I suppose there will be such a big crowd in town I won't be able to find a parking place."

"Don't we all wish."

"It doesn't hurt to wish, honey." He smiled, gave her a friendly salute and went out the door.

His words plucked at her conscience. She shouldn't have asked him to the picnic. They had gone out together a few times since that winter day he had promised to go sledding with her and hadn't. He'd explained later that he had had car trouble, and he'd taken her out to dinner to apologize. There had been movie dates after that, but Raine determinedly kept things on a light, friendly basis and Doug was not an insensitive man. He knew she wasn't ready for a deeper relationship. But Raine sensed that he was waiting with a calm determination that arose out of a stronger feeling than friendship.

She was wrong to encourage him, she knew that. Yet he made her life a little more tolerable. He made her forget Jade, at least for a few hours. But when she returned to her room with Doug's light goodnight kiss on her lips, thoughts of Jade haunted her. She lived on a roller coaster of emotion that peaked each Saturday morning when Jade brought Tate to the house and slid downward that evening when the vision of his lean body, his hard cheeks and his firm mouth rose up to taunt her. She would lie in bed and try to shut out the memory of his hands on her body. But she couldn't. She could only remember how it felt to have him touch her, and how much she ached to have him touch her again.

The day of the picnic dawned bright and sunny. As a member of the Commercial Club, it was her job to help.

At eight o'clock that morning, she found herself one of a crew of a dozen people who were faced with feeding a crowd of what they hoped would be close to five hundred. She looked up at the sky. Thank God it didn't look like rain. The blue prairie sky was cloudless and there was a light breeze.

On a grassy area in front of the swimming pool, under the shade of tall oaks, one of the men had set up a huge tent. That was a start. But they needed the heavy wooden tables moved. John Rossow, the president of the club, delegated Raine to solve the problem. She cajoled other members of the club to work in groups of four. Together, her improvised crew dragged the tables over the grass to form a semicircle facing the tent opening.

After that, things started to fall into place quickly. Harry from the Bar and Grill had volunteered to cook five hundred hot dogs. He also provided, for a fee, five hundred single-portion bags of potato chips and the five hundred cans of soft drink that were cooling on ice. Potato salad and fruit salad and greens were to be brought by several families in the area. There were treats for the children, bags of salted peanuts and helium-filled balloons, to be distributed by one of the men in clown costume, who had not yet arrived.

The children began to come, clustering around the activity like bees to a hive. Tow-headed boys of ten tried to check out the grill, while girls who were a little older showed their sophistication by standing back and giggling. To distract the curious ones from the fire, Raine suggested they begin blowing up the balloons and handing them out. John made an exasperated gesture and told her to go ahead. Tom Dugan had rented a bottle of helium gas, and after a few minutes of instruction, Raine learned how to use it. Soon baubles of colorful balloons bounced from strings tied to the arms of the younger children.

One of the older, more mischievous boys in town approached her. Todd Anderson often ran free in the streets and one day he had come bursting into the print shop and frightened Julia. Raine had very firmly asked him to leave and not come back again. "Can I have a balloon?"

She resisted the urge to correct his grammar and filled one. "Here," she said, handing him the string and the balloon. "You're old enough to do this yourself."

He took the balloon, but something about his eyes bothered her. They swept her with a sly furtiveness that was far too cynical for a boy his age. She told herself not to be so unforgiving and was getting ready to fasten another balloon to the machine when he said, "I don't think I can do it. Will you help me?" He held out the balloon and pointed to the string which was now tangled around his arm. She stepped around the gas container and said, "Here, you just—"

In one quick move, he grabbed her by the nape, shoved the balloon in her face and released the neck. Helium shot into her mouth and nose. Too startled to have the presence of mind to strike his hand away, she ducked her head, but not before she inhaled a substantial dose of the gas.

Todd turned to run, and was snagged in mid-flight by the back of his collar.

"What's going on here?" Jade's voice was rough with anger.

"Nothing. I didn't do nothing."

"Don't lie to me. I saw. Apologize to Miss Taylor."

"I didn't do nothing—"

"Apologize," Jade said in an even softer tone.

Todd looked at Raine and mumbled, "I'm sorry."

"Louder," Jade ordered.

"I'm sorry," the boy said with belligerent resentment.

"Do something like that again," Jade said with soft emphasis, "and I'll see to it that you're very sorry—right where you sit."

"You don't scare me."

"You're all kinds of courageous, aren't you, pulling

tricks on young women. Do you frighten small children and old women, too?"

The boy flushed scarlet.

"A real man doesn't have to prove he is one." Jade released his hold on the boy's shirt. "Remember that."

Todd pulled at his shirt in a silent protest at Jade's indignity. "I don't need a big macho man like you telling me what to do."

"You obviously need someone."

"I don't need nobody." The boy said something more under his breath and turned to walk away. Jade made no move toward him and the boy melted into the crowd.

"You didn't need—" Startled, she stopped talking. Her voice was high and distorted.

"You got a good dose of that stuff. It's affected your voice." He grabbed her hand and hauled her away from the bottle of gas and toward the tent. Inside, John Rossow stood behind a table yelling at Harry about something. Jade cut him off in mid-sentence. "Get somebody else to blow up the damn balloons. Raine got an overdose."

John stopped yelling at Harry and turned to stare at Jade. "She's the one who wanted to do it in the first place."

"Well, she's changed her mind," Jade said, and before John could reply, Jade pivoted on a booted heel and took her out of the tent with him, leaving John standing there, muttering things under his breath.

He held onto her hand and tugged her into the shade of a tree. "Breathe," he ordered.

She thought about it for a moment, made a real effort to do what he had told her to do—and discovered she couldn't. The thought tickled her.

"I can't." Her voice was a squeak, her chuckle high-pitched like a child's. It was all incredibly funny and she had to laugh. Helplessly, she gave in to the urge.

"My God, you're high. Take a deep breath. Get it cleared out of your lungs."

"Can't," she said, shaking her head, laughing helplessly. "Can't breathe. Can't do . . . anything." She collapsed back against the trunk of the tree, still laughing.

Jade eyed her with a worried look that was totally unlike him. Still chuckling, she fought to keep her eyes open and try to identify that look. He frowned, his brows furrowing in a look of sheer exasperation. No, not exasperation. Frustration. That's what it was. Jade Kincaid was faced with a situation he couldn't control and he didn't like it, not one bit. The thought sent her into another paroxysm of high-pitched laughter.

"Raine, for God's sake." He grabbed her arm, mumbled an expletive that was a favorite of his, and began to walk with her away from the crowd and toward the print shop.

"Jade, don't," she managed to gasp out between spasms of laughter. "Let go of me."

"A walk will do you good," he muttered, and continued to drag her along at a fast pace that was almost too much even for her long legs.

"Jade, don't." Another gasp of laughter. All her restless nights and lonely days spilled out in this stream of laughter. The helium destroyed the facade she had hid behind for months and all her pent-up emotions came tumbling out. "Jade, you're so funny. Please don't frown like that. I . . . it makes me laugh."

"I'm glad you find me so amusing." His hard, annoyed tone of voice struck her as hilariously funny and she was off again.

Nothing in Verylon was very far from anything else and in seconds they were in front of the print shop. She had left the door unlocked, and Jade opened the door and whisked her inside. He guided her around the desk and pushed her down into her swivel chair. "Stay there. I'll get you a drink of water."

The idea tickled her. "That won't help, Jade."

He stopped suddenly, his broad shoulders in the middle of the doorway that led to the rear of the room.

With slow deliberation, he turned around. "Then maybe I'll have to try something else."

Slowly, purposefully, he took a step toward her. She put out her hands and between fits of laughter said, "No, Jade, don't. It's broad daylight and everyone saw us leave. They'll know we're . . . together."

He took a step. "Ask me if I care." His eyes gleamed green in the sun that streamed through the big glass windows.

She shook her head, but even the threat of his closeness couldn't stop her laughter. She put her hands up and what should have been a barrier became just what he needed to pull her out of the chair and into his arms. He bent his head and instinctively, lovingly, she tilted her head to meet his lips. "Jade," she breathed softly into his mouth.

"Raine," he answered in a throaty male husk that mocked and imitated in an amused way. A glint of humor flashed in the dark eyes and then his lips settled over hers, their strength and warmth so familiar, so wonderful that her laughter died away, and in its stead, passion rose, swift, sweet passion, curling upward from within to make her want more than just the touch of his mouth on hers.

His mouth lifted from hers. Giddy from the effects of the helium and his kiss, she murmured, "Your cure isn't working. I feel more lightheaded than ever."

"Then you'd better lie down." His mouth curved upward and, in the next second, he had swept her off her feet.

She clutched his shoulders. Being in Jade's arms was sheer heaven. "I'm not that lightheaded . . ." but even as she protested, she snuggled her head against his chest.

He carried her through the doorway to the back and laid her gently on the cot. In the daylight, she could see every play of expression across his face. He looked supremely male, supremely satisfied with himself.

The realization of where she was, and what had

happened the last time she was there with Jade, washed over her like a cold ocean wave.

"Jade, we can't . . ."

He leaned over her and took her mouth quickly, stopping her words, thrusting his tongue into the honeyed hollow that waited unguarded for him. The sweet, hot probing made her moan deep in her throat. Her hands reached out to push him away and, instead, touched his shirt and greedily sought the hard flesh underneath. Her own brief outfit of denim shorts and a T-shirt offered little protection from his seeking hands.

Her murmurs of protest faded into soft little moans of pleasure as his hands traced the shape of her breasts over the thin cotton.

"It's always the same when I touch you, isn't it, honey? No matter how much time goes by, no matter how long it's been since we've seen each other, it's always the same." He buried his mouth in the soft hollow of her throat. "Raine, I need you. I—"

The bell on the print shop door tinkled. "Raine?"

Jade swore under his breath with a vehemence that made her smile. "This certainly has a monotonous regularity about it."

He eased himself away and she sat up—but not in time to get off the bed before Doug Martin walked into the doorway. He saw them and halted, his expression a mixture of embarrassment, chagrin and anger.

"I've been looking for you," he said in a hoarse voice. "I thought something was the matter. Someone said you'd gotten a dose of helium."

"I did," she said quickly, too quickly. "I . . ." She got to her feet, faced him and tried to recover her poise. "Jade thought I needed . . ." she stumbled to a stop. Silence was better than a manufactured explanation that wouldn't have made any sense anyway.

"I saw what he thought you needed," Doug said, and it was the first time she had ever heard his voice tremble with anger. To Jade, he said, "She's going back to the picnic with me."

"Is she?" Jade's drawl was dark and dangerous.

"She's my date."

"But a moment ago she was kissing me, and very willingly, too."

How arrogantly sure he was of her. She couldn't let him think he had absolute power over her. He wasn't the only man in the world. And she had asked Doug to come. She had an obligation to him, not to Jade. "Stop it. Stop fighting over me like two dogs over a bone." She turned to Doug. "I'm . . . ready to go back to the picnic now."

Doug's eyes flickered over her, lingering on her mouth. "Maybe we ought to take a rain check." He turned away.

"Doug, don't go, please." He hesitated and then turned back, a guarded look on his face. Knowing she had hurt him, raw-edged from the height and swoop of her emotions in the short space of the morning, she said, "Please wait."

Beside her, she felt Jade's body tighten with tension.

Doug looked as if he was unsure whether to go or stay.

"I'm going with you," she said to him firmly and stepped to his side to follow him out into the street.

All the way to the park, with Doug making wary, light conversation, she kept her mind blank, refusing to remember the wanton way she had responded to Jade's kiss and the shuttered look in Jade's eyes when he had watched her go. When she and Doug reentered the park, there were a few curious glances directed her way, especially from people who had seen her with Jade earlier. She linked her arm in Doug's, put on a plastic smile and moved through the crowd. But she couldn't put Jade out of her mind for long. Tate stood beside Julia, the string of a helium balloon attached to his wrist.

He saw her and broke free from Julia's hold to race toward Raine.

"Look, Aunt Raine. Grandma Julia got me a balloon.

She said you were with Daddy." The boy peered quizzically up into Doug's face. "Where is he?"

Tate looked over her shoulder and his worried look dissolved into relieved happiness. "There he is. There's my daddy." Tate struggled out of Raine's arms and raced away over the grass toward Jade.

Raine straightened, standing squarely before Julia. Julia's eyes were curious, but she only said, "Everything all right?"

"Of course." Conscious of Doug beside her, she said, "I suppose I'd better find out what I should be doing."

"Yes, come on," Doug said, and smiled. "I'd like to see you working for a change."

"I'm always working," she protested lightly, turning, smiling up at him, and coming face to face with Jade. For a moment, his eyes bore into hers, and there was an emotion in the green depths that she had never seen there before when Jade looked at her. It wasn't desire. It was something entirely different. She'd seen him look at Tate that way occasionally, and she'd decided it was male pride in having a son. But why he should look that way at her, she didn't know.

Disturbed, she reverted to formal politeness. "Excuse me," she said coolly to Jade, taking Doug's arm and walking away toward the tent.

John, who by now was looking considerably more harried than he had an hour ago, directed her to work with Harry, stuffing hamburgers and hot dogs into buns. She went to stand behind the grill, and was put to work at once. Doug stood close by cheering her on with silly witticisms. She saw Jade turn his head and look at her for a moment. Then he swung away to walk with Tate to a fenced-off area where the games had been set up.

Throughout the day, she seemed to be functioning on two levels. One part of her laughed and talked with Doug while she worked. The other part of her was vividly aware of Jade, of the height of his tall body above the rest of the crowd, of the way he held his son's hand, of his patience as he participated in the ring toss with Tate.

In the afternoon, after everyone had eaten and the adults sat around on blankets or in chairs, lazily enjoying the shade or the sun, there was an ongoing schedule of games, foot races, bag races, tag with variations. Raine sat at a wooden picnic table and munched on a cold hamburger. It was the first chance she had had to eat and relax. But somehow, a family group had developed around Julia's table that included Tate, Marc, Sandy, Doug . . . and Jade. She was totally unable to control the tension that kept her back ramrod straight as she sat on the picnic bench in the empty spot left beside him.

The conversation flowed along lazily. If Doug felt self-conscious, he didn't show it. She wished she had the same ability to sublimate her emotions. She felt Jade's presence as if he were touching her physically, although he wasn't. He sat just close enough to look natural, and just far enough away to avoid brushing against her, the rolled-back sleeves of his light tan shirt exposing strong, tanned arms resting on the table.

"Business picked up any?" Doug asked Julia casually.

The older woman shook her head. "Not so you could notice it."

Jade was instantly alert. He gazed at Julia, who sat across from him, her hands folded on top of the table. "Has the school closing hurt you?"

"Indirectly. Matt's talking about selling out and going to a larger town. We really can't afford to lose his ad revenue," Julia said quietly, in what Raine knew to be the understatement of the year.

"I hadn't heard that." Jade sounded thoughtful.

Julia's mouth curved. "It's not the kind of thing we advertise."

On the other side of Jade, Tate wriggled restlessly on the bench. "Daddy, can I be in the bag race? Please?"

Jade tilted his head to look down at his son. "Aren't you a little young?"

Tate favored his father with an imitation of Jade's faintly sardonic look. "Five-year-olds can be in it and I'm seven."

"Are you?" Jade smiled. "I'd forgotten."

"Can I?" Tate begged. "I've been practicing."

"Have you?"

"Sure." Tate propelled himself off the bench, clenched his hands at his sides as if he were holding the edges of a bag, and hopped around on the grass like a jackrabbit, his pale hair flying.

"I can see you've developed your own style," Jade drawled. "Well, go on then."

Tate let out a whoop and ran for the tent where the bags were being dispensed.

"He is too young," Raine said, when she could hold it in no longer. "He could fall down and get hurt."

"That's a chance he has to take," Jade answered smoothly.

Raine cried, "He could break a bone . . ."

"For heaven's sake." Sandy peered at them from the other end of the table. "You two had better compromise on how you're going to raise that child . . . or you'll give him a complex."

"I won't have my son afraid of his own shadow."

"No," Raine grated. "He mustn't learn to show any human emotions like fear, or pain, or vulnerability."

There was a tense, awkward silence at the table. Then Jade said in a tone that was far more amiable than she probably deserved, "He'll have a thousand-acre ranch to run someday. If he doesn't learn the discipline of riding out on days when he doesn't feel like working, how will he survive?"

She didn't have an answer to that.

Doug moved uneasily on the bench across from her. "There has to be a compromise somewhere along the line. Men don't have to be tough every living minute of the day. They should be able to relax when they're at home with their women."

Jade's answer came back instantly. "That depends on the woman. Did you have a particular one in mind?"

A crackling silence followed Jade's words. Her appetite gone, Raine put down her half-eaten hamburger. Desperate for some kind of distraction, she looked past Doug's shoulder. "They're starting the race."

"Get ready . . . get set . . . go!" John bellowed the words, and from behind a ribboned line, people began hopping toward the edge of the park. There were a dozen contenders of all ages in the race. Tate was not first, but neither was he the last. And he hadn't fallen.

The race over, Tate ran back to the table, his eyes shining. "I did good, didn't I?"

"You did just fine," Jade assured him.

Preparations were being made for the three-legged race. There weren't many contenders and John began to hustle the crowd.

"Come on, folks. It's excellent exercise. Who's going to enter? We've got a dandy prize here for the winners."

Doug grinned at her. "Are you game?"

She hesitated, and in that beat of quiet, it seemed to her that everyone at the table waited to hear her answer.

"Sure, why not?"

Fighting to hide her reluctance, feeling Jade's eyes on her as if they were branding her, she rose from the table and followed Doug to the side of the tent.

There was already a curious crowd gathering where the contestants were being tied together at ankle, calf and thigh with striped red, white and blue ribbons.

"You gonna participate?" John blustered at her, "Well, I can't tie you together when you're standing three feet apart. Step up close to him, Raine, and put your arm around his waist."

In full view of most of the population of Verylon, she was forced to do as John asked, fitting her body into the side of Doug's. His arm went round her and his hand clasped her hip. Just at that moment, in her peripheral vision, she saw Jade join the watching crowd.

Quickly, with impersonal hands, John tied the ribbons at their ankles, calves and thighs.

Doug tightened his hold on her waist. "I'll try not to outreach you. Let's see if we can get a rhythm established."

It was awkward, but not as bad as she had expected. Doug was not that much taller than she and he compensated skillfully for his longer length of leg. He moved when she did, making slight adjustments to his stride to ensure her balance.

Together, using a rhythmic gait they seemed to establish quite easily, they reached the starting line. At their arrival, the watching crowd quieted.

"Trust me," Doug said softly.

She turned her face up to his and smiled. "Is there any reason why I shouldn't?"

"Sometimes," he said under his breath, "I wish there was."

She laughed softly and turned to face forward and get ready for the race. Across the top of several heads, her eyes met Jade's.

His face looked as dark as a prairie thundercloud. Before she had time to wonder why, John bellowed the starting words once again and they were off.

"Move in strict rhythm so I know what you're going to do," Doug instructed.

Out of an instinctive need for self-preservation she obeyed. She had no desire to make a wrong move and pull him down on top of her.

They found a swinging stride that suited both of them. Raine watched as other couples who had started off faster lost their rhythm and tumbled to the ground. Soon there was no one in front of them. They swung along together, Doug urging her on under his breath. "Just a few more feet."

The foot fastened to Doug's caught on a rough spot in the grass and she lost her balance. She fell, taking him with her.

He reacted instantly, twisting to put his body underneath hers. His quick action pulled her on top of him. She lay sprawled over his chest in an abandoned carelessness that looked anything but innocent. Doug laughed up at her, his eyes sparkling with enjoyment, and moved his hips suggestively underneath her.

"You have an evil mind," Raine chastised him.

Doug threw up his hands and lay back on the grass. "You're the one who threw yourself on top of me."

Conscious of the crowd watching, Raine struggled to get up. She couldn't. Jade stepped out of the crowd and his hard hands caught her shoulders. "Wait a minute."

His touch was not calming. She writhed within his hold.

"Raine," Doug breathed, his face flushing brick red. She stared at him, suddenly aware that her movements had inadvertently heightened his sexual awareness of her and that he wasn't any happier about it than she was.

A knife clicked. Jade stooped beside them and began to cut the ribbons at their ankles.

That done, he proceeded to the tie at their knees. At the last ribbon, his fingers brushed the soft inner skin of her upper thigh. She couldn't conceal the shudder. He saw the tiny goose bumps and his mouth tightened. Grimly, he went on loosening their fetters, until at last she was free.

He picked up the ribbons, sliding them over his lean fingers. His eyes played over her and then shifted to Doug. "You might want these for a souvenir." He let the red, white and blue strips of satin go, and they fluttered to the ground at Raine's feet.

8

The hot summer days dragged by. September came and went, and the sharp October air in Verylon turned smoky with haze as people raked leaves and burned them in trash barrels behind their houses.

The week before Halloween, Raine had a visitor in the print shop. As the bell jangled, she looked up and for a moment her heart stopped. The tall figure silhouetted in the door was Jade's height. The figure moved and came into the room.

"Hello, Raine."

Her heart began beating again at a slower pace. "Hello, Marc." She leaned back in her swivel chair.

"Are you . . . busy?"

"Not particularly." She waited, watching him. "Sit down." She indicated a straight-backed chair at the side of her desk.

He shook his head. "I'm not going to stay that long. I just . . ." He paused, his eyes guarded. "Oh, hell. I know it's none of my damn business, and I wouldn't be here if Sandy wasn't . . ."

He stopped. "Do you know what's wrong with Jade?"

She tried to meet his eyes without betraying her own shock. "Is something wrong with him?"

"He's acting like a horse with his foot caught in a prairie dog hole. Sandy was the one who noticed that he's always worse on the days he brings Tate in to you."

Her heart began to race again. She struggled to frame a cool answer. "I can't imagine why. We don't exchange more than two words."

Marc gave her an anguished look. "Well, whatever it is, it's getting to him. He doesn't eat enough to keep a bird alive, let alone a grown man, and he isn't sleeping much, either." He gave her a straight look. "I thought you two had something going there for a while."

She looked away from him, down at the galley she had been proofing. The words blurred in front of her eyes. "I told you then you were wrong."

He leaned forward suddenly and put his palms flat on the top of her desk. "I don't think I was. Not about you and Jade. But I . . ." He straightened away. "I sure regret what I said about my brother to you that night. I wish to hell he would find a woman." He thrust an anxious hand through his hair. "He doesn't do a damn thing but work. He works till ten every night and gets up at five. At the rate he's going he'll be dead before he's forty."

She clenched her fists in alarm. "I'm sure that whatever is bothering Jade has nothing to do with me."

"There was a rumor going around for a while that you were planning to marry that other dude. Are you?"

Raine lifted her chin. "I'm not planning to marry anyone."

"Can I quote you on that?"

"What are you going to do?" she asked coldly. "Explain to Jade that we had a little talk and that I'm still . . . available?"

Marc looked stricken. "My God. He'd knock me flat on my face if he thought I was trying to sell you on him."

"And if you say anything to him about me, I'll do the same."

He shook his head. "What can I do?"

"Nothing." She stood up. "There isn't anything anyone can do."

Marc took a breath and said in a growl, "You can't tell me he doesn't love you. He was looking at you at that Fourth of July picnic like he wanted to eat you alive."

She caught her breath. "That's absurd!"

"And I think you love him."

The lie came out quickly. "I don't."

Marc shook his head. "Things can't go on like this forever."

"They can and they will. There's nothing between us, Marc."

He lifted his head and stared at her. "You two are the most stubborn fools I've ever seen." He stomped out the door.

She watched him go, her knees shaking so badly that she thought she would fall down. She gripped the desk with both hands and sank back into the chair. What was wrong with Jade? *He's always worse on the days he brings Tate in to you.* Was he angry because she was so much a part of Tate's life?

Marc's words haunted her, kept her lying awake nights. She knew she had to do something. She just didn't know what.

On the next occasion that Jade brought Tate to her, he said a perfunctory hello and turned to go just as he always did. But this time, she put out her hand to catch him. He wore a short-sleeved shirt and as her cool fingers settled on his arm just below the elbow, he made an involuntary movement, as if she had startled him. She pulled her hand away, but not before she saw the dark, leaping flame in his eyes.

"I'm sorry," she said at once, and then wished she hadn't as the crease on the side of his mouth deepened from the slight lift of his lips.

"You don't have to apologize for touching me."

She curled the fingers that still carried the memory of

his hard flesh into her palm. "Is it a hardship for you being away from Tate every Saturday?"

He leaned away from her slightly, balancing his body on the heels of his boots. "What's the matter? Are you tired of your 'lifetime commitment' already? Or is Martin complaining?"

She flushed angrily. "No. I just . . . I just didn't know if you were still . . . happy with our arrangement."

"We've established a routine now." He glanced over at Tate. The boy raced around Julia's pocket-sized yard and jumped into a pile of leaves. His dog followed. Tate's animal friend was no longer a puppy. The full-grown collie was almost as tall as Tate and had a beautiful thick coat of burnished copper and a plumy tail that waved in perpetual motion. "It might be hard to explain to Tate why we're making changes."

"That's true," she admitted. "I just thought that—"

"Tate is with me almost constantly," Jade murmured. "I need a day away from him as much as he needs a day away from me. If you were a single parent, you'd understand that."

"You mean you really are human after all?"

"You of all people should know just how human I am." He took a step toward her.

Sobered, she shook her head. "Don't play games with me, Jade."

"What makes you think I am?"

Determined to keep it light, even though her heart racketed in her chest, she said, "It can't be anything else with you."

"And you don't want to play?"

For an agonized moment she was tempted to cry, *Yes, yes, I do, more than anything in the world.*

"No." A blink of the eyes, a tightening of her fingers in her fist were the only signs that betrayed her. Her voice, when it came out was cool and dry. "I think I'd better get Tate in before he ends up in the rosebush."

His green eyes raked over her in a look as cool as her

voice had been. "I wonder if Martin knows how lucky he is."

Desperately afraid a small movement of her body would betray how little she cared about Doug's mythical luck, she turned and walked away from him over the grass to Tate. "Come on, buddy. Grandma Julia made some sugar cookies for you."

She didn't sleep well at all that week, and on the next Saturday, when Jade came in to make the arrangements to pick up Tate at the end of the day, she would have said something to him, she wasn't sure what. But his manner was cool and impersonal and the words died on her lips. The same thing happened a week later. The week after that she gave up, thinking that Marc had an overactive imagination. There were other things to occupy her mind. The *Verylon Appeal* was gradually but surely going bankrupt.

Caught up in Christmas preparations, Raine tried to put the disastrous financial state of the newspaper out of her mind. On Christmas Day, Julia presided over the table that was laden with food as if she had nothing more pressing to worry about than lumps in the turkey gravy. She had asked the entire Kincaid clan for Christmas dinner, and they all came, Sandy, Marc, Tate and Jade. Raine managed to be busy in the kitchen most of the time, and at the table she divided her attention between Tate and Sandy. After the turkey was eaten and the dressing praised and the traditional complaints about the full states of their stomachs had been made, they went into the living room and sat around the tree to unwrap their presents. Sandy, her cheeks flushed, looked down at Tate, playing with the new wooden tractor that Raine had given him and said, "Marc and I are going to be parents."

Marc turned a bright shade of red while Julia beamed. "When?"

"Somewhere around the 1st of May," Sandy said proudly.

"Congratulations," Jade said softly, his eyes on Sandy.

Her color deepened. "We thought we were going to wait but then we . . . decided not to. There didn't seem to be any reason to put it off."

"I'm so happy for you," Raine told her and gave her a quick hug.

But later, when she went in to the kitchen to tackle the stack of dishes, Jade came up behind her. She steeled herself, totally unprepared for his hand to slide along her arm and pick her left hand up out of the soapy dishwater.

"No Christmas ring?" he asked softly.

She wrenched her hand away, leaving a trail of soap bubbles on his arm. "What business is it of yours?"

"Are you going to live with him instead?"

She swung around to face him, her eyes blazing. "I repeat, it's none of your business."

His eyes gleamed, and she was sure he meant to say something sharp and perhaps uncomplimentary. He made a convulsive movement with his hands and then stepped back. "You're right, it isn't."

After everyone left and Julia had gone to bed, Raine sat in the living room, staring at the tree. The luster of the Christmas lights seemed to dim. In a few months, perhaps less, Julia planned to close down the paper and sell the shop. What would she do when that happened? Julia had assured Raine that she was welcome to stay in the little house. But how could she do that with no funds? She had to find a job, and it had to be somewhere in eastern South Dakota.

Yet how could she stay and face an increasingly hostile Jade? For Tate's sake she must. If she didn't, there was a good chance he would grow up learning to dislike and distrust women as much as his father did.

A few weeks later, during a January thaw, she had an

idea. If she could somehow buy the equipment on time from Julia, she could turn the print shop into a place that did work on commission. She might be able to garner some printing business from out-of-state. The thought captured her imagination and grew stronger as the winter days passed. She thought about it all through the blustery frigid days of March. Then one day in April, when she sat in the print shop at her desk and looked down at the sheet of figures she planned to present to Julia that night, the phone rang.

"I wonder if you'd be able to take Tate on Friday rather than Saturday," Jade's low voice said in her ear.

When she realized who it was, her mouth went dry. It was the first time she had talked to him on the phone in months. "I don't see any reason why I couldn't."

"I wouldn't ask, but I need to drive to Canton to get some legal business done and the offices aren't open on Saturday."

"It's no problem, Jade. I can take him. He can come here to the print shop with me."

"Are you sure he won't be any trouble?"

She curbed the rise of impatience and kept her tone level. "I'm sure."

A silence hummed over the telephone wire. "I have it on good authority that the paper is folding."

His cool unconcern rankled. "As soon as Julia is finished with her advertising obligations, she's going to stop publication."

Another long pause. "Have you made any plans?"

Why did he care? "No."

"You'll be leaving Verylon."

Suddenly she knew the truth. He was questioning her because he wanted her to leave. Her temper flared to life. "You're very anxious to get rid of me."

His answer was smooth. "There's no work for you here."

He was actually pushing her to leave! She fought sick disappointment with anger. "You shouldn't have let me *see* how anxious you are to have me go. You don't usually tip your hand in advance like that, Jade. Hasn't it occurred to you I might stay just to annoy you?"

He said a short, succinct word, and the clipped sound pleased her. She'd gotten under his skin. She burrowed deeper. "Summer's coming. You hire extra help, so does Frank Radley," she said, naming another rancher whose land holdings were only slightly smaller than Jade's. "You could probably use an extra hand right now, before the college crew arrives. The town's still complaining that you haven't fixed that fence. I can string barbed wire or herd cows and haul bales if I have to. I used to do it for you for nothing." She paused. Only half in jest, she said, "Would you . . . hire me, Jade?"

Silence simmered in her ears.

"No."

The clipped word stung. He wanted her to leave. He couldn't have made it any clearer. She covered the hurt with a flip tone. "Well, that takes care of one job interview. Let's hope Frank is more broad-minded than you are."

"Is that what you think I am? Narrow-minded?"

"If I were a man, you'd hire me without a second thought."

"If you were a man, I wouldn't have to worry about sending you out on the range with other men."

"I can take care of myself."

"The way a snowflake takes care of itself on a hot stove. . . ."

Quickly, without thinking, she hung up. Half expecting the phone to ring immediately, she got up from the chair, went into the back room, and picked up the kettle to hold it under the faucet. The phone stayed silent, and in the silence, she seethed. Why did he think she would melt in any man's arms?

Because you did in his.

The kettle overflowed. She jerked it away and slammed it down on the little two-burner stove so hard that the table holding the stove rocked. He didn't care if she fell into another man's arms, not really. He hadn't given her a job because he didn't want her to stay in Verylon. He wanted her to leave. Why? Because she was getting too close to Tate or because she reminded him of Michele? Once he had kissed her and held her in his arms. But that had been so long ago. He hadn't touched her since the day of the picnic. It was obvious he no longer wanted her, even in a physical way. He didn't seem to want or need a woman at all. He hadn't taken any more trips to New York, and he hadn't been seeing Natalie. Sandy had mentioned that she thought Natalie's husband wanted a reconciliation. If what Marc said was true, Jade was living the life of a monk, his days taken up with his work on the ranch and caring for Tate. While she . . . she lived without the ease her body craved. During the day she managed to forget, but at night, her mind and heart still remembered the touch of his hand on her breast. She decided to put off talking to Julia for another week.

On Thursday, she had a surprise visitor. She hadn't seen Doug in months, but he didn't seem self-conscious about the length of time that had passed. Within minutes he was perched on the corner of her desk, talking as easily as if he had never been away.

"Ad business still bad?"

"Nonexistent."

"Maybe you ought to do what this other editor of a small-town paper did. He created his own want ad business." Doug waited, watching her. She leaned back in her chair and said in a measured voice, "And how, she asked with bated breath, did he do that?"

Doug grinned. "Went out one night and opened all the stock gates. The next day the roads were full of cattle and the telephone in the newspaper office rang off the wall with calls from ranchers wanting to place notices in the lost-and-found column."

Raine grimaced. "I don't think that would go over too well here."

"Why not? You could start with Kincaid's gate. His pasture is close to town. With a little help in the middle of the night, Verylon could be another Pamplona."

"With young bulls running rampant through the streets? No, thank you. Doesn't sound like our style. Besides, Jade doesn't have any young bulls. He only raises steers and heifers."

"Too bad. This town needs something to liven it up."

"Maybe, but cattle on the loose wouldn't be my first choice."

Doug slid off the desk and cast an eye over her hands. She had picked up a pen and was toying with it for lack of anything else to do.

"Somehow, I thought I'd see a ring on your finger by now."

The pen slipped from her fingers. She fought the urge to laugh hysterically. Where were all these rings she was supposed to be wearing? "Why did you think that?"

He shrugged. "Kincaid isn't exactly an invisible man. He's known around the territory. Scuttlebutt in Canton says he's winding up his divorce."

"How could you possibly hear something like that?"

"Several ladies over there have been following the proceedings with, shall we say, an interested eye?"

The thought that Jade was no longer legally tied to Michele, that he was free to be with any woman he wanted and marry her if he chose to do so, jolted her with the force of an electric shock. "A mercenary eye, perhaps?"

"From what I've heard Kincaid has more than just his money to make him attractive to women." His leg stopped swinging as he twisted to face her. "You seemed rather 'interested' yourself last summer."

She swiveled in her chair and the protesting creak of old wood filled the quiet in the shop. She kept her eyes on her hands, on the bare finger that would never wear Jade's ring. "That was almost . . . a year ago and it didn't mean anything. There's . . . nothing between us."

"I guess seeing isn't believing then. The way he was leaning over you, I thought I'd walked into the middle of a seduction scene."

Desperate to stop him, she said lightly, "You think entirely too much, you know that?" Then, quickly, to divert him, she asked, "Would you like to come to the house for lunch? Julia just made one of her famous ice-water chocolate cakes."

For a moment, he looked tempted. Then he shook his head. "I'd better not. I've got to finish the rest of my run."

He gazed at her for a moment. "I really came just to say goodbye. I'm being transferred to a route in the Minneapolis, St. Paul, area."

Her sense of loss surprised her. "That will be a promotion for you, won't it?"

"Yes." He stood with his hand on the doorknob, his eyes locked with hers. "Raine, you're at a dead end here. There are more job opportunities in a city. If I asked you to come with me, would you consider it?"

She shook her head. "Don't. Please, don't. You've been a good friend, but . . ."

Now he shook his head. "Spare me the good friend routine, Raine. Listen to me. There's nothing here for you. You should leave this place, come to the city with me . . . live your own life for a change."

The phone rang, and Doug gave the instrument an impatient look. "Well, answer the damn thing," he said in a rare burst of impatience.

"I may have to cancel my trip," Jade said immediately into her ear, and the strangely unsettled tone took away the shock of hearing his voice and made her focus her concentration on what he was saying.

She said, "What's wrong?" and knew the tone of her

voice had betrayed her when Doug shot her a curious look.

"It's Tate. He can't understand why I'm leaving him with you tomorrow instead of Saturday. I had trouble getting him to go to school today and he's determined not to go tomorrow. He wants to go to Canton with me."

"Don't give in to him."

"I don't want to, but I . . ."

She could almost see the twist of his mouth, the frustrated look in his eyes. "He probably thinks you're going to go away . . . too."

"I've told him that I'll be back."

"He doesn't believe you. He needs something to take his mind off worrying . . . something he can look forward to in school. Wait, Jade, I've got an idea. Let me work on it and I'll call you back."

She hung up the phone, and began to dial again, almost forgetting that Doug was still there. But his cool voice stopped her hand in midair. "So Kincaid's not interested in you, huh? I must say I admire his technique. He strings you along with a few kisses and gets free babysitting."

"That's not true . . . you're wrong . . ."

"Well, it won't be the first time. I sure was wrong to think he might do the decent thing and marry you. Well, what the hell. I might as well make another mistake." Resolutely, he walked around the desk, and before she could move away, he bent his head and kissed her soundly on the lips. "That's for good luck," he said softly. "I have a feeling you're going to need it."

He went, and she sat staring after him for a long moment, listening to the jangle of the bell. Was Doug right? Did Jade see her as a convenient baby-sitter? No, that was ridiculous. It had been her idea to keep Tate one day a week, not his.

She shook her head and marshaled her thoughts. She had another problem to solve right now. She reached for the phone to call the school.

She wasn't able to contact Tate's teacher immediately, but she left a message for the woman to call her and in twenty minutes, the phone rang again.

She explained to Mrs. Calhoon, the lively, older woman who taught second grade, what she had in mind. Mrs. Calhoon was delighted.

"That's a wonderful idea. I'd love to bring the class down to the print shop tomorrow. Could we come in the morning, say around ten-thirty? The children are always fresher then."

"Ten-thirty is fine."

Later, after supper, when Julia had gone to bed and she sat alone in Julia's living room watching TV, the kitchen phone jangled.

"I want to thank you." Jade's voice had that deep, husky sound that was so familiar to her. "I don't know what you did, but it worked. Tate wants to go to school tomorrow."

"I'm glad."

"I'll be bringing him in to the shop around eight."

"Fine."

She waited for him to ring off, but he didn't. After a second or two of silence, he said softly, "Is anything wrong?"

"No." She said the word quickly, too quickly.

"Raine." It was a soft protest, an invitation to tell him the truth. Even though their communication in the last several months had been minimal, he knew instantly that she was lying. "Have you been working too hard?"

Her laugh was not amused. "Not particularly."

"Is . . . Julia all right?"

"She seemed a little tired and she went to bed early, but other than that, she's fine."

Stop probing. I don't want your concern.

"You sound as if you could use some rest, too."

"I suppose I could."

Another long pause. "Is that a polite request for me to let you go?"

"If you haven't anything more to say . . ."

His voice cooled. "Goodnight, Raine."

She hung up, knowing why she had been short with him. She had rejected Doug's words intellectually, but they had gone below the surface of her mind and lodged there. Jade was free now, free to love again, marry again. How long could she go on loving him and receiving nothing in return but telephone calls about his son and brief glimpses of him when he dropped Tate off? How could she bear to watch him go out with other women?

A few minutes later, in her room, she undressed and got ready for bed, knowing she couldn't put off a decision about her own future much longer. If she decided to buy the print shop equipment from Julia on time, she was committing herself to several years stay in Verylon. But if Jade married another woman—she couldn't bear to stay. And if he married someone after she had committed herself to a large loan for the Linotype and press, she would be caught here until she found someone to buy the ancient equipment and take over the payments. She could end up trapped in Verylon, with no way to escape to look for a job in Canton or Sioux Falls.

She lay down and fell into an uneasy sleep. Endless, ridiculous dreams chased round in her head, dreams of Tate and Jade and cattle on the loose.

A soft April rain began and ended in the early morning hours. Through her restless sleep, she heard it drumming on the roof. She didn't think of the consequences of that rain then, but later, because of the April shower, there were fifteen pairs of rubbers and boots to be unbuckled, unzipped and loosened when the second grade class descended on the front step of the print shop promptly at ten-thirty.

Raine went from one youngster to another, offering help. Some of the children were quite self-sufficient, while others clearly wanted assistance. Tate quietly took off his own boots and shrugged out of his yellow raincoat. When the slickers and jackets were piled on the old-fashioned coat rack near the door, Mrs. Calhoon shepherded the children into a semicircle around the Linotype machine.

Raine settled into the chair and swiveled around to look at the children, whose curious eyes were on the same level as hers. Tate stood directly behind her and the expression in his dark eyes might have been Jade's. She tore her eyes away from Tate and began. "Before printers had machines like this one they set type by hand on a composing stick." She held up the ruler-type wood made with a back and a movable brace to keep the letters in place. "Mrs. Taylor and I don't do that. We use the Linotype to make the words your parents read in the paper." She smiled at them. Their eyes were bright and wide as they looked at the Linotype. "Today I'm going to make lead slugs of the most important words in the world. What do you think those words are?"

"Our names," Kevin Harson shouted with an exuberance that won him a quick, sharp look from his teacher.

Raine smiled. "That's right, Kevin. And do you know what I'm going to do with those lead slugs when they're finished?"

"Give them to us," Kevin shouted again.

Behind her, Mrs. Calhoon murmured, "It's really better not to ask them too many questions."

Raine smiled and nodded, and immediately asked another question. "Can everybody see the keyboard?"

Choruses of yes, yes, answered her.

"I'll use a key from this side," she pointed to the right side, "for the first letter of your name and I'll use these letters," she pointed to the left, "for the rest of the letters. You probably call the ones over here capitals. Once, long ago, when printers set type by hand, the capital letters were kept in the upper part of a case like a pyramid." She touched her fingertips together to demonstrate the shape of the case. "A printer would call out to his apprentice 'upper case E' and that meant he wanted a capital letter. We still call capital letters 'upper case' and small letters 'lower case,' even though we don't use cases to keep our letters in any more. Kevin's name starts with this letter here," she located the capital K in the fourth row down, second from the right on the keyboard. Kevin beamed.

"Once I turn the machine on, it will be too noisy for me to talk. Do you have any questions?"

"When can I see my name?" Kevin asked.

"Right now," Raine said, smiling.

She swiveled around, knowing that out of the fifteen pair of bright eyes, it had been Tate's she was most conscious of. The machine began its rattle and bang and soon Kevin's name came sliding out. Each child had written his or her name on a card and Raine watched those cards and tapped out the correct letters. In minutes, she finished the last name and turned off the machine.

"My name looks funny." Kevin was clearly disappointed.

"That's because it's the mirror image of itself. Let's put some ink on it and see what happens."

She went to the marble table, swabbed the lead letters with an ink dauber and pressed it on the large sheet of paper she had prepared for the purpose. She held up the paper for Kevin's inspection. He grinned.

She was besieged by voices saying, "Do mine, do mine." One by one, she inked each name and pressed it on the paper, explaining that this process was called letterpress printing.

When she did Tate's and handed it to him, he accepted it gravely. It was a revelation seeing him with his class. He seemed quieter, more controlled. His resemblance to Jade was overwhelming. On an impulse, she asked Tate for his name, made an imprint of it and held the paper up for the rest of the class to see. "Notice that Tate has two 'T's in his name and part of those t's come above the a and the e. That part is called an ascender. Tammy on the other hand," she turned to a blue-eyed girl standing next to Tate, "has an ascender and a descender. See how the y comes below the line?"

"Why did you tell us that?" Kevin asked, his eyes tightened into a squint.

"I just thought you might be interested in how each letter is different, just as each of you is different."

"Oh." Kevin subsided and clutched the lead letters that spelled his name inside the paper Raine had wrapped them in.

Later, after the children were shown the press and the paper folder, they got back into boots and slickers and trouped out the door.

"Thank you," Mrs. Calhoon said to Raine, as she stood just inside the door. "You've sharpened their interest in letters and words immensely. Reading is going to be much more interesting to them from now on. I only hope I can answer all the questions they're bound to think up when we get back to school."

"If you think I could answer them, give me a call." Then she added lightly, "I wasn't being altogether altruistic, you know."

"You've been a real help with Tate, Jade tells me."

Raine kept her voice casual. "I suppose I'm trying in a small way to undo the damage."

"Last fall, I wouldn't have thought that was possible. I worried about Tate. But now, he seems quite . . . content."

A cry went up from one of the children out on the sidewalk. Mrs. Calhoon raised her eyes heavenward. "I'd better go. Thanks again."

Doug had told her that casting the names of the grade-school children in type was a tradition in newspaper offices around the country, but she had never done it before. She wished she had. This would be the last year there would be schoolchildren in Verylon. It would also be the last year she would be working in the print shop—if she didn't do something about it.

Seeing Tate with his classmates had been enlightening. He'd matured so much in the last year. She wanted to be here to watch him grow, to see him turn into a man with

Jade's integrity and fortitude. She had to stay. She'd tackle Julia about buying the Linotype and the press as soon as possible.

She had no chance to talk to her aunt that day. It was Friday and the children's visit had put Raine behind schedule. The time flew by and suddenly it was three o'clock and time to collect Tate from school. Since Raine was the Linotype operator, the task fell to Julia.

"Don't come back here," Raine told her. "Take him home and give him his snack and milk. I can finish up here by myself."

Julia looked doubtful. "Are you sure?"

"Yes, I'm sure. If I get a couple of uninterrupted hours, I'll have this done by five-thirty." Julia agreed and hurried out the door.

Raine had just finished typesetting the last page and turned off the Linotype machine when she heard the bawl of a calf. She shook her head. She must be hallucinating. She carried the heavy galley over to the marble table and was leaning over it, scanning its backward letters when she heard a calf bawl again. She raised her head and looked out the window. There, out in the street, several Hereford calves ambled lazily; they were the nearly full-grown kind that Jade would soon be sending off to market.

It wasn't a stampede, it was an invasion. A curious steer was poking his nose at Harry's screen door and another was cropping the small tree Raine had planted in a square planter in front of the shop.

"Here, you get out of there." She opened the door and waved her arms. The steer merely raised his head and gave her a long, unbelieving stare and went back to eating her tree. His companions had found other trees to sample. She opened the door. A quick look down the street told her there were at least fifty head of cattle on the loose. Some of them were grazing on the grass in the park, their hooves marring the turf softened by last night's rain. John would be furious. She swore softly under her breath and ran back through the still-open door into the shop to pick up the phone with shaking hands.

"Sandy?" She remembered Sandy's condition and forced her voice to a lower level. "Where's Marc?"

"He's over on the old MacKinsey place plowing."

"All right, thanks."

"Is anything wrong?"

"A couple of Jade's calves are on the loose and wandering around town," she said in what she knew to be the understatement of the year. "Maybe I can get Harry and a few of the men around to help me get them back behind the fence."

"I can page Marc . . ."

"Do that. Although by the time he gets here we'll probably have everything under control." A bellow came from across the street. She glanced out the huge front window. Harry, roaring, exploded out of his establishment to stand on the street and swear at the top of his lungs at the hapless cattle, as if he could make them disappear by the very force of his shouting. At the same time, from the opposite end of town, Jade's pickup raced up the street. The commotion startled the steer who was making a meal of Raine's tree. His head came up. Panicked, he bounded for shelter—straight through the door of the print shop.

She had the presence of mind to hang up the phone. She stood up from her relatively safe place behind the desk and told herself there was nothing to be afraid of. But herding an eight-hundred-pound steer from the back of a horse was not the same as facing him nose to nose in the confines of a room.

"Now you just turn right around and get out of here," she told the wide-eyed animal.

"What the—" Jade burst into the room. The startled calf jumped, galloped past the Linotype machine and squeezed through the doorway and into the back room.

"Now look what you did!" Raine cried. "Oh . . ." An ominous crash followed. Fury overriding her initial trepidation, she ran into the back room. The steer was investigating the spilled sugar cannister, lapping the white grains.

Infuriated, Raine waved her arms and charged the intruder head on. "You get out of here."

She was snatched by a hard hand that clamped over her shoulder like a vise. "Stop scaring him to death unless you want him to do a lot more damage to the place than he's already done." He looked down and grimaced at the muddy tracks on the wooden floor.

For the first time, she looked at him, really looked at him. He wore a soft suede suit in camel brown and a creamy lawn shirt. His facial skin was smooth and faintly scented with a woodsy male cologne. Jade hadn't been so close to her in months and he hadn't touched her in what seemed like an eternity. "Let go of me," she said huskily, "and concentrate on getting your livestock out of here." Desperate to be away from Jade before she betrayed her clamoring reaction to his closeness, she tugged free of his grip, startling the steer.

The animal's head came up. His hooves clumped on the floor and he was off again, running in a frenzied circle. He staggered into the small table that held the stove and sent the stove crashing to the floor. He did a clumsy bovine dance to regain his balance and lurched against the cot. One of the legs on the frame collapsed and the bed tilted crazily.

Raine cried, "No!" Her voice sent the steer into another agitated gyration.

"Get away from the door," Jade roared. "Let him through."

Raine jumped away. The steer bounded through the doorway—and ran headlong into the press. The crank snapped off and clattered to the floor and the electric cord whipped from the wall, crackling with sparks. The blank pieces of paper awaiting the running of the press flew loose from the tray and scattered into the air like snowflakes.

Her only thought to get the animal out before he burned the place down, she ran at him. He turned and dodged around the Linotype machine, tripping over its heavier, ropelike cord, which popped loose from the socket with a crackle and hiss. The ends wrapped around the animal's hock and sent him sprawling, wedging him behind the Linotype, his legs bowed outward like the warped legs of a table.

Raine erupted with fury. Reason gone, vengeance uppermost in her mind, she picked up the push broom and brought it down on the calf's back. The calf could only dodge his head from her clumsy brandishments.

"Get out of here, you stupid animal. Get out!"

The calf gathered his legs under him and scrambled desperately to be away from this apparition with an instrument of death in its hands. The wood floor was slippery with the mud from his hooves, but he got to his feet and raced to safety on the other side of the Linotype machine away from Raine. She threw the broom down and ran after him. Behind her, Jade gave chase.

They circled the machine once, then again. "Raine," he roared. "Raine! Stop!"

He grabbed her shoulders and brought her hard up against him. "Stop acting like a crazy woman and use your head. Get over behind the Linotype and keep him from circling again. I'll try and head him toward the door."

His hands on her shoulders brought a shuddering reaction that stilled her. He didn't seem to notice. "Go on, get over there."

The calf came round again and halted wide-eyed in front of Raine. Jade thrust her to one side, stepped directly in front of the excited steer and caught the animal's ears. "You crazy fool! Get the hell out of here."

The calf reacted to Jade's voice and touch on the tenderest part of his anatomy by lowering his head and shaking it hard. When that didn't loosen Jade's grip, he braced his feet and charged, butting Jade into the wall. Jade lay pinned and helpless between the hard head and the wall.

Jade's breath wooshed out of his body in a low groan. Raine cried out in horror, "Let him go! *Jade!*"

Raine's cry of terror startled the calf, and he raised his head. She flung herself at the animal's rear, grabbed his tail and jerked furiously. The calf turned his head to peer owlishly at this new menace.

"Raine, for God's sake. Get away!" Jade's attention was divided and the calf, sensing it, gave one violent twist of his head, shook himself free of Jade's iron hold, scrambled around, and in a burst of speed, ran straight out the door.

In the sudden silence, Jade turned to her and took a step toward her. "Are you all right?"

His quiet concern for her increased the trembling relief she felt at seeing him upright and apparently unharmed. "I wasn't the one he knocked against the wall. Are you all right?" In the aftermath, her knees trembled. He could have been seriously injured.

"I'm used to dealing with stupid cows." He moved closer, eyeing her. "Are you telling me the truth? Do you hurt anywhere?"

She laughed nervously and gestured around the room with her hand. "Only when I think of how much work it will be to clean this up."

"Don't worry about the shop. I'll make it right."

She couldn't bear to let him see how shaken she was about his tussle with the calf. "If you don't get out there and round up the rest of your herd," she told him, the mud stain down the front of his expensive jacket triggering her sense of the ludicrous humor of it all, "you won't have anything left to make it right with. Your cattle are ruining John's park and if you don't get them out of there, he might decide to have a steakburger barbecue on the Fourth of July this year, compliments of you!"

A smile tugged at the well-cut mouth. "He might at that."

"Come on," she said, tugging at the sleeve of his jacket. "Get that fancy coat off. We've got work to do, cowboy."

"We?" Jade's tone was dryly amused.

She walked through the open door and into the sunshine. Jade followed. Gesturing at the portion of his herd that stood grazing in the park, she said, "See what I mean?"

Jade looked, swore, and strode into the street, forgetting about his good clothes.

Harry had already made some progress, turning most of the herd back from the east part of town. He stood in the middle of the road and bellowed at the cattle, which, Raine thought privately, would be enough to scare anyone, man or beast. She and Jade set out on foot, threading back and forth, gathering the herd into an unwieldy bunch and getting them moving in the direction of the range.

Moments later, on the outskirts of town, the last calf went through the gate and Jade swung it shut. He ran his hands over the post and then examined the wire loop. "I'd sure like to know how in hell that gate came open." He fastened it securely, slipping the loop over the post. "Nothing's been broken. From the looks of things, somebody came along and deliberately opened it."

A tingle of alarm went through her. "Who would do a thing like that?"

"Somebody who had a grudge against me, obviously."

He relaxed back against the post, his lean body moving easily under the supple material of his clothes. The late afternoon sun gave his hair the patina of antique gold and his eyes a dark, devilish twinkle. Against a blue sky just tinged with a touch of purple, his tanned face stood out in stark, clean lines, the planes of his cheeks taut and masculine. The fresh smell of earth and grass and Jade mingled to tantalize her nose. For a man whose stock had just run rampant through the town, he looked very much at ease, almost . . . happy. He said, "I'll have an electrician out to fix those cords tomorrow."

"That's a start," she said, staring at him and unable to tear her eyes away. She hadn't seen him in such an amiable mood in years. Whatever, or whomever, he had seen in Canton had done wonders for him.

He met her gaze with the unselfconscious ease that was characteristically his, his lips lifted in a dark, attractive smile. "What's the matter? Do I have dirt on my nose?"

"On your suit," she said, lifting her hand to brush it away and snatching it back before her fingers made contact with his body.

He caught her hand in midair. "Don't be afraid to touch me."

"I'm . . . not." She pulled at her hand, but he didn't release it.

"Have dinner with me." His smile deepened and showered her with Kincaid charm. In this mood, he was irresistible.

That charming smile and his hand holding her fingers made it difficult for her to think. He was dressed to the teeth and he'd been to Canton. A man didn't dress like that just to go see his lawyer.

"No, I . . . I'd better get home and see about Tate."

"He's all right with Julia. I've already spoken to her."

She raised silvery eyes to him. "When?"

"I went to the house first and asked her to keep Tate while we go out."

"You were very sure I'd go."

He said impatiently, "Of course I was sure. Raine, we . . . have to talk."

About what? About the wonderful woman you've found? About how much you appreciate what I've done for Tate but now you've found someone else to act as his surrogate mother? She shook her head. "Send me a postcard."

He stared at her for a moment as if he couldn't believe she'd said those curt, cutting words. "Raine, listen to me. I . . ."

For almost a year, she had fought with her longing for him. He had treated her with indifference. Now, he'd found someone else and he wanted to tell her about it. She couldn't bear it. "Whatever it is, I don't want to hear it. I'm not . . . not interested in anything you have to say."

With a suddenness that startled her, his amiability fell away. His face as dark as a Dakota storm sky, he grasped her hand and pulled her close. "Listen to me, you little fool. I've got something to explain to you and I don't intend to say it out here with a bunch of cattle watching."

The brush of his hard body on her own sent her over the edge. "Stop manhandling me as if I were one of your cows."

"If I thought it would help to grab you by the ears, I'd do it," he muttered hoarsely.

She struggled and pushed and writhed in his arms. His hard grip was unyielding and in her own desperation to get away, she twisted her arm too vigorously. She cried out in pain, and instantly, he let her go.

She rubbed her injured wrist.

"I'm sorry," he said coolly.

"It wasn't your fault," she admitted honestly, more anxious than ever to be away from him. The glittering green of his eyes kept her rooted to the ground. Fighting to bring herself back to reality, she said, "You'd better check your fences before you go away the next time."

"Thank you for the advice, Miss Taylor." He dipped his head and then raised it to gaze at her, a burning anger in his eyes. His voice was cool, utterly unconnected to those furious green depths. "I presume you'll send me a bill for damages."

"You bet I will." She turned to go, aware that he stood utterly still behind her and that his eyes were on her as she walked away.

"Isn't Daddy coming to get me soon?" Tate asked at the supper table, his eyes turned first to Raine's face and then to Julia's.

"No, honey. You're staying all night with me," Julia soothed him. "Your daddy had some work to do and he thought he'd get it done more quickly without you."

"I'm a good helper."

"I'm sure you are," Julia said, smiling. "Maybe your dad thought you needed a little vacation after a hard day at school." Julia nodded to the lead type that Tate held in his hand and said in an undertone to Raine, "He hasn't let go of it once since he came in the door."

Her mouth twisted. "I'm glad something good came out of this day."

"Is the shop really bad?"

"If Jade has the electrician come, that will take care of the worst of it, I guess. The back part really suffered more damage than the front . . . well, maybe not. The whole place . . ."

". . . looks like it's been bombed," Julia said, smiling, quoting Raine's words of a moment ago.

"I don't know how you can take it so lightly."

Julia raised eyes that were clear and untroubled to Raine. "I'm sure it can't be too bad. . . ."

Raine stared at her. "I know you're not going to publish the paper any longer, but that equipment does represent an investment."

Julia set the fine china cup she was holding carefully into its saucer. "Raine, I have to tell you something. I should have told you weeks ago, but I was afraid that . . . you would somehow take it badly."

"Take . . . what badly?"

"I've sold the print shop."

"Sold . . ."

"The building, the equipment, everything. We made the transaction two weeks ago. I've been renting the place from the owner for the last two months."

Her stomach felt as if she had just taken a ride on a roller coaster. She heard herself asking in a comparatively normal voice, "Who . . . bought it?"

Julia picked up her cup. "Why, Jade, of course."

"Jade? Jade bought it?" A heat rose in her cheeks.

"Yes, why not?"

"What's he going to do with it?"

"He plans to sell the press and the Linotype to a printer in Iowa and use the building as a distribution center for another feed company he's bought to turn into a co-op."

"Why didn't you tell me?"

"I didn't think it made any difference to you. You knew the paper was closing down. You'd already mentioned you were planning on driving to Canton to look for work."

She stared at Julia. "I was going to offer to try and keep the shop open. I thought if I got job printing I could . . ."

Julia shook her head. "I thought you might try something like that. I mentioned it to Jade, and he agreed with me that it wasn't a good idea. You'd only go more in debt, Raine."

Raine clenched her teeth together and fought to absorb the impact of Julia's words. The truth came in a flash of pain. "He couldn't wait, could he?"

"What are you talking about?"

Tangled emotions roiled through her. "He couldn't wait to get rid of me."

Julia looked totally taken aback. "My dear! I'm certain that wasn't his intent at all. Jade was only thinking of me."

"How convenient. But when he helped you, he helped himself, didn't he? He solved all his problems at once."

"What did Daddy do?"

Raine looked down at Tate. She had almost forgotten he was there. Julia shot her a warning look. "We'd better discuss this some other time. Tate, let's go up and have a bath now, shall we?" To Raine, she said, "We can talk more after I've tucked Tate in."

Raine shook her head. "I'm not questioning your motives."

A strange look flickered over Julia's face. Then she said calmly, "Well, if that's the case, perhaps you'd better drive out and talk to Jade now, while Tate is here with me. You can clear up any misunderstanding without worrying about little ears listening."

"Maybe I will," Raine said, her anger flowing through her like a warm stream. "Maybe I will just do that."

9

Her fury escalating, she got into her car and headed out of town. The gravel roads were still wet from last night's rain, but in spite of the dampness, loose gravel pinged into the undercarriage. She drove fast, her anger making her less cautious than she should have been.

There was no one around when she pulled into Jade's yard. His foreman lived in a house down the road a few miles and she supposed he had gone home for the night. A few determined steps took her to his front door. She stabbed at the doorbell and then half-turned and tapped her foot in a staccato rhythm against the brick stoop. Nothing happened. She gave the doorbell another poke, holding it down with her finger. Through the door, she could hear the chimes repeat their melodic summons. She turned to scan the buildings nearby. Was he out on the range somewhere or doing some repair work in the machine shed?

Behind her, the door swung open.

Jade stood there, wearing nothing but a terry coverup that began at his waist and reached his knees. Amber hair clung damply to his cheeks and nape, and the light covering of darker whorls on his chest held drops of moisture. His body exuded a faintly soapy smell.

"Do you always answer the door in . . . that?" She gestured toward the half-robe he wore.

"Yes," he said coolly, "and the phone too, when I've just come from the shower." He took her arm, drew her into the house and shut the door, acting as if her sudden appearance on his doorstep was the most natural thing in the world. "Here, let me take your jacket." His hands went to her shoulders.

"I won't be staying that long if you're getting ready to go out." Had she been unconsciously hoping he would deny it? He didn't.

His mouth moved upward in a half-smile. "No problem. She's coming here. I've made a fire. Go on into the living room. I'm still on the phone, but I'll be with you in a minute."

He divested her quickly of her jacket before she could protest and gave her a little push toward the luxurious conversation pit. Then he strode away to the kitchen, making any further protest useless. Her anger dissolved. A welling sickness took its place as she walked woodenly over the plush carpet.

Jade's fire crackled in the fireplace and filled the room with warmth and welcome but even with the distraction of listening to the fire, she could hear Jade murmuring in a low intimate tone to someone on the phone. No wonder he was sure he had plenty of time. He was still talking to her. Were they so much in love that they had long, intimate telephone conversations before spending the evening together?

In spite of the warmth, a chill shivered over her arms. Did she really have the courage to stay and watch some other woman make her home here?

Jade's soft laughter drifted into the room and the sound of it made the muscles in her stomach tighten in pain. Yet what right did she have to deny him his happiness? Surely he had suffered enough with Michele. If she, Raine, loved him . . . truly loved him with the only kind of love that was worth anything, the kind of love that put his happiness above her own, she should be glad he had found someone to take the agony out of his eyes and the bitter twist from his mouth.

She couldn't tarnish Jade's happiness. It didn't matter what his motives were for buying the print shop. No matter what he thought or did, she was staying. But they would have to reach some kind of truce, because of Tate.

She jumped to her feet and climbed the two steps out of the conversation pit—only to hear Jade hang up the phone.

He was in the doorway before she moved two steps. He walked toward her, his bare feet soundless on the soft carpet. "Where are you going?"

One moment he was three feet away from her, the next he had hold of her arm. "Come and sit down."

She went with him, suddenly anxious to say something, anything, and leave before the woman he was seeing arrived.

He pressed her down into the soft cushions of the couch and sat next to her, his terry coverup parting slightly, exposing his knees and a portion of his hard upper thigh. "What did you want to see me about, Raine?" he asked pleasantly. "Did you think of something more you wanted done at the shop?"

"I . . . no. But the shop . . . the shop is why I'm here. I . . ."

She tried to keep her eyes on his face, but she seemed unable to see anything but the bare satiny skin stretched tautly over his shoulders, the bare skin of his upper arms, the muscles well-molded underneath, the nakedness of his thighs covered with the hair that was several shades darker than that on his head. She tried again, but her throat had gone very dry. "I . . ." a remnant of her temper returned and in her distress, she blurted, "Why don't you go put some clothes on?"

"Am I bothering you?"

She fought the urge to cough with nervousness. Dear God, what a question! Bother wasn't the word.

"We know each other well enough for certain . . . intimacies." He picked up a strand of her long hair and played with it, wrapping it around a lean finger. "Don't you think?"

Think? She couldn't think at all. The gentle tug on her scalp that signaled his possessiveness overwhelmed her. Her only defense was to say what she had to say and get out of Jade's house as quickly as she could. "Julia told me today that you . . . you bought everything."

"Did she?" His fingers tangled in her hair and brushed her shoulder. "Did that upset you?"

"Yes. I know . . ." She took a breath and tried to block out the subtle seduction of his fingers in her hair. "I know why you did it."

"Do you?" He dropped the strand of hair he had been fondling. Relief mingled with disappointment until her overtaxed nerves registered the fact that he had moved closer and was sliding his arm around the back of the couch behind her. "Why did I do it?" He bent his head and his mouth moved to the side of her ear. His warm breath whispered over her skin.

"To get rid of me," she murmured, every sensible part of her brain telling her to move away, every cell in her body refusing to deny the pleasure of that warm mouth nibbling around her ear.

"Did it work?" he breathed softly.

His failure to give her even a token denial stung. "No," her voice trembled, "it didn't. I'm not going anywhere." His tongue touched her ear lobe. Panicked, she pulled away. "I'm staying," she said staunchly, more to convince herself than Jade. "I'll have to drive to Canton to find work, but no matter what you do, I'm not leaving. This is my hometown and I belong here and I . . . I won't go." What should have been an angry denouncement came out in a breathless rush.

"So you're not leaving town?" His tongue circled closer, probed deeper.

She cried, "Don't!" The anguish in her voice must have penetrated. He pulled away in surprise.

"No. I'm not leaving town." Her anger fueled by her pain, she twisted to face him head on and blurted out exactly what she was thinking. "How can you do this to me when in a few minutes, another woman will walk through that door?"

He laughed softly. She cried out and tried to get up but he covered her shoulders with his hands and pushed her back into the cushions, half-leaning over her, trapping her under his hard body. "Anyone who walks through that door during the next twelve hours takes his life in his hands." The gleam in his eyes and the suppressed violence in his voice told her that he meant every word.

She tried to make sense out of her whirling thoughts. "But . . . you said you were waiting for a woman . . ."

"I was." His eyes caught and held hers. "I've been waiting for her for a long time. And now that I've got her," his hands tightened slightly on the word, "I don't want any interruptions." For a long heady moment, he simply gazed at her. Her eyes wide and dark, she stared back, breath held.

For an eon, he held her, until she felt the tension in his body as if it were in her own. When he saw that she was waiting too, watching him with silvery eyes that were alive with hope, but still waiting, he shook his head ruefully, made a sound that was a half-laugh and bent his head. His mouth came down on hers gently. The restrained warmth of his kiss, the hard intensity of his hands, and the controlled passion of his body told her that there was no other woman in Jade's life.

All doubts vanished. She was the woman he wanted, the woman he needed. All her years of silently loving him focused on this one blinding moment. She exploded in a blaze of relief and ecstasy under him and strained upward to meet his kiss, her mind and heart and body alive with an all-consuming hunger. He felt her need and moved to satisfy it, coming down on her more heavily, his body laying half on hers, his mouth taking hers with a hard passion that betrayed his desire. She moaned softly. Afraid he had hurt her, conscious of her slenderness trapped under him, he lifted his mouth and moved to ease himself away. "Oh, please," she murmured, "I . . ." She caught herself, realizing that she was begging him to lie on top of her.

He read the expression on her face and ran a teasing finger over her nose. "It's all right, honey." His other hand moved under her back so that she lay cradled between his arm and his body. "From now on you can say anything you want to me"—his mouth moved over her face, covering it with featherlight kisses while his voice dropped to a lower, huskier, more amused tone— "do anything you want to do."

"Anything?" she breathed, touching his bare back, dancing her fingertips lightly over his spine from the nape of his neck to the indentation of his waist above the terrycloth.

He groaned in her ear. "Where did you learn that little trick?"

Sobered at once, she struggled under him. "Jade, I can't . . ."

He lay on top of her, clearly enjoying her efforts to free herself. Her movements made her breasts rub sensuously against his bare chest and at her slight intake of breath, he smiled, the devilish highlight in his eyes reflected by the firelight in the rapidly darkening room.

When she stopped trying to get up and lay exhausted he brought his lips down to her mouth and said, "What can't you do?"

"I don't . . . I've never . . . I've always loved you," she said in a desperate whisper next to his mouth. "I read all the books. I knew I should . . . should try to find someone else to . . . to make love to me because you were out of reach. But I couldn't. I couldn't bear the thought of making love with anyone else."

The hard muscles of his body tensed. Then he said in a low, husky tremble she hardly recognized as his voice, "I . . . had hoped. But I was sure that you couldn't possibly still be . . . untouched."

"I won't know what to do," she whispered miserably.

"And you'll be self-conscious about yourself every minute of it, won't you?" He lifted himself away and rose. She ached with loss, but even while she was steeling herself to meet his disappointment at her inexperience, he swept her into his arms.

"First of all, honey, we start with the proper atmosphere." He climbed the two steps out of the conversation pit, crossed the room and bore her up the short flight of stairs that led to the upper story. "And that means going into the bedroom and closing the door," he said, suiting his actions to his words, kicking the door shut with his bare foot. Inside the room, he smiled down at her. It was a smile filled with desire, promise and a protective possession that thrilled her. "Because here," he paused to let his eyes move over her slender body, "we have both privacy and comfort, two important requirements for making love."

Love for him welled up inside of her. "Jade . . ."

He covered her mouth with a brief, hard kiss, making her forget what she had wanted to say. Longing rocketed up from within her and while she was grappling with her reaction to his mouth devouring hers, still kissing her, he let her slide down the length of his hard body to stand on her feet.

"The next thing we do is get you into a tub of hot water."

She smiled in surprise. "I think I'm already in hot water."

He laughed. "You haven't even begun to get into trouble, Miss Taylor."

"Oh, I think I've begun," she said as his hands went to the top of her blouse. She caught them, resisting.

He chuckled, his eyes caressing her. "You can't get in hot water until you take your clothes off."

She cast a dry look over his half-naked body. "Is that the theory you subscribe to?"

He laughed again and cupped her face in his hands, his thumbs probing and finding an exquisitely sensitive spot under her ears. "It's not a theory; it's fact."

"One you've tested enough times to know."

His smile faded and his hands dropped away. He pulled back emotionally and shut his thoughts away behind an impassive face. She knew suddenly, with great clarity, that he was steeling himself to hide pain. "I can't erase my experience with other women—or with Michele. I can't tell you that I didn't love her. I did. But it's over. Today, I'm free, legally, morally and emotionally. But I can't wipe out the past. If that bothers you, you'd better walk out that door." His eyes burned over her.

He took another step backward, creating an intolerable distance between them. She hadn't known she could feel such pain. She hadn't meant to accuse him or open old wounds. Stricken, she stood staring at him.

He said coolly, "You have to make that decision." A muscle on the side of his jaw moved as if he had clenched his teeth. "But for God's sake, have a little mercy and make it quickly."

The tortured quality of his voice swept away her doubts. Swiftly, she stepped to him and pressed her lips against his cheek. "Jade. Please forgive me. What happened in the past no longer matters."

He stood still, not touching her, letting her put her arms around him. Then his hands came up and he folded her into a hard embrace. "Thank God," he said with such heartfelt intensity that she knew he believed her. "I was almost afraid to hope. I've been lying awake nights, wondering if marrying the wrong woman would keep me from having the right one."

Having, not marrying. Her heart stopped for one moment. But there was no going back. She was committed to Jade on whatever terms he wanted her.

"Now, where were we?" he asked softly, holding her, rocking her slightly in his arms, his low amused tone telling her he knew exactly where they were.

"We were getting me into hot water."

His grip on her loosened fractionally. "Ask me to undress you, Raine."

She had fantasized this scene a hundred different times, in a hundred different ways, but now, faced with reality, the low, sexually arousing words made a wave of shyness sweep over her. She buried her head against his chest.

With a gentle hand under her chin, he tilted her face toward him. "You don't want me to undress you? All right," he said, swinging her up into his arms. "We'll do it your way." He carried her through to the bathroom and set her on her feet, still holding her as he turned on the water.

In minutes, steam wafted into the air. But he made no move to do anything other than hold her at his side as he tested the water and added a silky softener from a green bottle. She stood beside him, trying to fight down the nervous tension that made a hard knot in the pit of her stomach.

When the tub was nearly full, he knelt at her feet. She was wearing soft black cotton shoes with buckles, and in seconds, he had them off and was removing her stockings as well.

In the steamy heat of the bathroom, she could feel the tendrils of hair curling around her face. She looked down at the lean, male body bent in front of her. The same heat made the blond tendrils at Jade's nape loosen and curl inward, the antique gold curls a bright contrast to his bare shoulders with their look of sinewy copper.

He rose and encircled her in his arms. But instead of undressing her as she expected him to do, he shifted his grip and swung her off her feet and into the air, turning her so that she was over the tub.

Laughing, a tingling excitement mixed with fear of the unknown, she cried, "Jade, what are you doing?"

"I want you to take a bath," he said, that dark smile deepening wickedly, "and you don't want to get undressed. So . . . we'll compromise."

Surely he wasn't going to put her in the bathtub with her clothes on. But he was. Slowly, inexorably, he lowered her into the water. "Jade, stop it. You're insane . . ." She laughed and kicked and pushed at his arms.

"If I am, it's because you've been driving me crazy for years."

The intensity in his voice shocked her into stillness. She lay in his arms, quiescent, and looked deeply into his eyes. "Jade. Do you mean that?"

"I never say things I don't mean." In that moment of her nonresistance, he lowered her into the water. "Oh . . . oh!" The warm wetness against her bottom told her she had reached the point of no return. "Jade!" She came to life and made one last valiant struggle to save herself, but it was too late. Laughing, pommeling his chest with her fists, she fought, but he was undeterred by the wild flailing of her arms and the restless motions of her legs that scattered water on his bare chest. He settled her into the tub, a dark smile on his lips. Fully submerged, her blouse clung to her breasts and her jeans tangled like wet ropes around her legs, hampering her kicking.

Jade eased his hands away, enjoying every moment of her distress, his dark green eyes gleaming with enjoyment. There was only one method of retaliation. With quicksilver speed, she cupped her hand and splashed water directly into his face. He sputtered, coughed and shook the water out of his eyes. "Why, you little devil." He leaned over the tub edge and lunged.

She tried to dodge away, but there was nowhere to go. In one swift move, he grabbed her wrists and pushed her against the back of the tub. She laughed and struggled against the pressure of his hands and tried to break away. "Jade, I . . ."

He lowered his head and kissed her with a mouth damp with the water she had tossed at him, his tongue thrusting into the sweetness she had unwittingly offered him. She resisted for a moment, but when the impact of his warm mouth began to send a sweet electric charge through every wet inch of her skin, she tipped her head to give him greater access. He probed with sensuous power, discovering every corner of her mouth. She gloried in his possessiveness and shuddered as his tongue took a circling tour of all the sensual delights of her honeyed sweetness. Then he retreated, and when she made a soft sound in protest, he kissed her again, opening his mouth to her and inviting her to reciprocate. When she didn't immediately accept the invitation, his tongue returned to tantalize and tease and slid away again, in a blatantly sexual game of come hither.

A bubble of laughter floated upward, and with it came the courage to answer his invitation to play. Her answering thrust was tentative at first, her tongue just touching the edge of his lips. But when he took her into his mouth with a soft, sucking motion, a violent surge of need tore away her inhibitions. She became the aggressor. Thrusting her tongue further into his mouth, she explored, retreated and returned to explore again until a guttural sound came from his throat. "Raine."

He made a move as if to pull away from her. She caught his shoulders to keep him from leaving her. "Undress me, Jade," she murmured against his lips, saying the words she had been unable to say a moment ago.

His hands went immediately to the pearl buttons on her blouse . . . and lingered there, his trembling touch betraying his eagerness and need. "Raine. I want you to be very sure."

She looked at him, her eyes gleaming silver. She

thought she had loved him before, but now, watching him give her one last chance to refuse him even while he trembled with desire, the well of love inside her spilled over. "I'm very sure. I've been very sure for a long, long time."

Under his expert hands, the wet buttons slid easily from their places. He pulled the tails of her soaked blouse from the waist of her jeans and slowly dragged one sleeve off her shoulder and down the length of her arm, his mouth following the wet cloth. When he had freed her, he tossed the dripping blouse into the sink. "Crazy woman," he murmured, pressing his mouth against the soft flesh of her chest just above her bra. "Whatever possessed you to get into the bathtub with all your clothes on?"

"The devil made me do it." Her fingertips danced lightly over his shoulders, showing him just exactly who her "devil" was.

"You really should learn to control yourself," he teased, as his hands went around her back.

"I should? I . . ." She gasped softly, for her bra was unhooked and the straps were pushed down over her arms by warm male hands. The wisp of lingerie went the way of her blouse.

His eyes burned over her and her body reacted as if he had touched her, her flesh swelling in warmth and readiness. But he didn't reach for her. Sure that she must have displeased him in some way, she said softly, "Is something wrong?"

"You're . . . too beautiful to touch," he said with a husky intensity that rocked her to the core. Inexplicably, he held out his hands to her, his eyes on her face. "Lift up, honey."

For a long, silent moment her eyes held his. Then, with a calm acceptance that told him quite clearly how much she trusted and loved him, she did as he asked.

Savoring the sweetness of her smile, he unbuttoned her jeans and ran the zipper down. She supported herself with a hand on his shoulder, and allowed him to strip the water-heavy denims from her. He tossed them on the growing pile of her clothing. Below the water, she was left in nothing but her sodden cream bikinis. "Again, sweetheart," he ordered, and they, too, were whisked away in a sliding, caressing movement of his hands that explored the entire length of her legs.

He went back on his heels, and she sat before him, letting his gaze wander over the darkened tips of her breasts just visible above the soapy water. In that instant of visual communion, she dared to whisper softly, "I know I'm not as beautiful as . . ."

He groaned. "You're more beautiful than any woman I've ever known. Any woman!" he repeated fiercely. "Do you believe that?"

She shook her head. "I . . . can't."

"Then I'll show you." He stepped into the tub and sat down behind her, pulling her shoulders back against his chest. "God, I remember how much I wanted you the night of your birthday party . . ." He dropped his mouth to her nape and nibbled her lovingly.

"Jade . . . your coverup. You're soaking it."

From behind her hair, he said silkily, "Then help me take it off."

When she hesitated, he smiled. "Believe me, it will be much easier than what I did for you." She twisted around to look at him, supporting her back against the side of the tub. He took her hand in his and guided it to the fastening at his waist. "There's only this small button here." He placed her fingers over it. She held back, not sure that she could accomplish even that small task with hands that were shaking from the pleasure of feeling his wet nakedness.

"Don't make me ask you again," he said in a low husk that vibrated with contained impatience.

She fumbled for a moment and then the button came free and she caught the half-robe and tossed it outside the tub to the floor. In a breathtaking instant, she knew he would never be more completely hers to savor. The aching loveliness of this moment was almost more than she could bear.

He clasped her shoulders and pulled her back against him again. "Tell me what you're thinking."

"I'm thinking," she breathed softly, "that I am the luckiest woman in the world."

It was just as she had fantasized, only better, much better. The strength of his thighs against hers, the warmth of his arms around her. . . .

"Lean forward," he murmured. When she did as he asked, he brought the heavy wet silk of her hair around over her shoulders so that it hung down and curled over her breasts. "I want to feel every inch of your lovely bare back against me," he muttered huskily.

When she nestled back against him, he began to touch her arms, learning the shape of her elbows and her shoulders. He explored the side of her neck, lightly flicking her earlobe with the tip of his finger. He toyed with a strand of her hair and rubbed his knuckles against her cheek. She lay against him, floating in the warm water, loving every stroke of the gentle caressing until a throbbing warmth behind her told her that though he was deliberately touching her in all the least provocative places, his detachment was due to his iron control.

"Jade, I . . ."

"Shh." From behind, his fingertips sought and found her lips. "We have all the time in the world."

He went on touching her for another endless eon. She enjoyed every minute of it, but she knew what it was costing him to prolong his non-arousing caressing. She made a restless movement.

"Are you getting cold? Would you like to get out?"

She nodded, ignoring the sudden pounding of her heart at the thought that once she was out of the water, her body was Jade's to see and to touch in any way he cared to.

He helped her out of the tub and as if he sensed her

fears, almost ignoring her as he dried her body with a fluffy towel and a brisk efficiency. But his impersonal manner wasn't enough to stop the rise of hot color to her cheeks when he knelt to dry her ankles and drew the towel gently up her slender legs to rub her inner thighs. She tensed, and he felt it. He glanced up at her and laughed softly, then straightened and wound a towel around her wet hair. When he finished, he handed her a dry towel, his face expectant.

"Be brave, Raine," he murmured, chuckling at her expression. Starting at his chest, she rubbed him down as she might have one of his horses. She gave his hips and legs the most cursory of rubbings and went quickly to his arms and back. He laughed out loud, snatched the towel from her hands, threw it behind him, and led her into the bedroom—to the bed. The hard sensuality of his body against hers made her lie down quickly and draw the sheet over herself.

To her surprise, her diversionary tactic wasn't necessary. He had turned away from her and naked, supremely unselfconscious, he strode around the room, turning off all the lamps but one soft light on the far wall beside his dresser.

"Did your bath relax you?" he asked, when he came back to sit down on the bed beside her, take the towel from her head, and brush her hair away from her shoulders as if he were in the bedroom to do nothing more than carry on a casual conversation.

"Not exactly."

His lovely naked maleness was a feast for her wherever she cared to look: taut throat, hard satiny shoulders, muscled chest, narrow waist, trim thighs, all covered with a light dusting of dark gold hair. Just below his elbow, his hip bone made a hard and uncompromising curve against skin that hadn't been exposed to the sun. Unable to resist the urge, she put out a finger and touched it. A tiny wave shuddered through his body. He caught her hand and brought her finger to his lips. "For someone who hasn't made love to a man before," he murmured, "you have an astounding way of zeroing in on all the right places." He pressed his lips into her palm.

"I don't know what's right and what's wrong," she whispered.

"Honey, there is no right or wrong between us. There's only a world of pleasure."

The husky assurance in his voice gave her the courage to say, "Jade, I . . . I want to give you pleasure, too."

He found the pulse at her wrist and touched it lightly with his tongue. "And I want everything you have to give."

She breathed in sharply as his tongue wandered lower and caressed the part of her palm where his lips had been. "Jade . . ."

He murmured softly, "Relax. Let me arouse you first, sweetheart. Believe me, it works better that way."

His unwitting reminder that he had made love to a woman many times before made her nerves tighten, but in the next moment, she had no time to think of anything, for he was drawing back the sheet from her body and sliding in to lay down beside her and lean over her. Cool air wafted over her and, in the next instant, his warm fingers traced the circumference of one breast and then the other, trailing a hot warmth and a heady pleasure over her sensitized skin. He traced and retraced a circling path where curved flesh rose away from her chest until she felt as if she were melting like snow in the sun. She hadn't known she could be so sensitive to the texture and pressure of a man's fingertips, hadn't known she could savor each tiny caress and yet be greedy for more.

"Jade . . ."

"What is it?" he breathed, leaning over her, gently tonguing the valley between her breasts.

"I . . ." In the next instant, his mouth covered a swollen crest, bringing a sigh of pleasure to her lips. She realized now that she had only glimpsed heaven that summer night so long ago in the rose arbor. Now, Jade's tongue flicked and teased and claimed and circled her taut bud, creating a symphony of delights. When her breath dragged through her lungs, he raised his head. "Is that what you wanted, Raine?"

Leaning over her, his green eyes gleaming, he aroused a feline, feminine reaction in her. The urge to have him in her power as he had her was overpowering. She reached out and flattened her palms on the silky chest hair that lay over hard muscles, sliding her hands over it, discovering the male nipples. Their hard buds told her that she was succeeding.

"Oh, God, yes," he breathed. "Giving, taking, touching . . . this is the way it should be. . . ." She knew instinctively that a part of his control had gone. Driven by a primitive urge she had always known Jade would release in her, she let her hands roam over his shoulders, the curve of muscle in his arm, the still-damp hair at his nape. Intent on her search to know every curve and muscle of him, she was unaware for a moment of where he was touching her . . . until she felt the weight of his hand on her abdomen and knew that he was reaching for the ultimate prize.

Her initial reaction was shock. He felt her tension and withdrew his hand—only to put a teasing finger in her navel and cup the other over her hip bone, arousing a wanton longing for his touch to return to that intimate place where a heated need was beginning to pulse.

With a wicked chuckle, he drew endless, looping circles over her abdomen, circles that encompassed the tops of her thighs. Round and round his hands went until she cried out for the lovely torment to stop—and to begin. And when he ceased his restless teasing and let his hand drift to that silken femininity again, she lifted her hips to accommodate his touch—and moaned when he gave her the pleasure he had promised would be hers.

He moved over her. "Honey girl, listen to me." His voice sounded strangely hoarse. "This is going to hurt but it will just be for a minute; trust me, trust me, my love."

She did trust him, but she couldn't tell him, couldn't do anything but be aware that the world was shifting, turning from pleasure to pain.

"Relax, sweetheart," his hands cupped her face, "you're doing beautifully . . . oh, so beautifully. God, I . . . ah, yes, now, Raine. Move with me . . ."

The world fell away and the pain receded and nothing remained but Jade. Slowly, gently, he began the exquisite journey of discovery. Warmth flooded her body and her mind. He murmured love words she had never heard before in her ear, words of encouragement and praise and adoration. His loving murmurs made a wellspring of feeling bubble up from deep inside—feelings that had never before been touched. And yet, those three vital words were missing. . . .

He explored her with infinite care, bringing her shades of feeling that swung from pleasure to a terrifying ecstasy. He was one with her and she with him and it was everything she had ever dreamed and more, so much more.

He lay beside her and trailed a lazy, questing finger around her breasts, down over her navel to circle over her abdomen. She looked at him drowsily.

He smiled. "Are you going to sleep?"

"Not if you keep doing that."

"Do you feel like talking?"

She considered it. "Not if you keep doing that."

He laughed and gathered her into his arms.

Afterwards, when she lay snuggled in the hollow of his shoulder, she said, "Jade, I'd better . . . go."

"You're not going anywhere."

"But Julia—"

"Julia knows where you are."

"But not that I'm staying—"

"I told her you'd be spending the night when I talked to her on the phone."

"You're very sure of yourself . . ." Realization dawned. "You mean that was Julia you were talking to when I got here?"

Amusement colored his voice. "Who did you think it was? Never mind, don't answer that. The same mythical woman you thought was coming to see me, I presume." He raised up and leaned over her to give her a punishing kiss, then trailed his hand over the soft skin below her throat. "I like you like this, in my bed, wearing nothing but a love blush."

"Jade! My clothes! They're soaked . . ."

"We'll dry them in the morning." The amused voice deepened. "You won't need them until then."

"Jade, I can't stay. People will talk."

"After we're married, there won't be anything to say."

The love haze fell away. It was wrong, all wrong. Because he didn't love her. "I can't marry you."

She felt the hard stillness of his body. In contrast, his voice was soft, too gentle.

"Why not?"

"It just isn't possible."

"What alternative do you suggest? An affair? Or should I just accept you as my live-in lover?" He paused, waiting. "That would be a little difficult to explain to Tate, don't you think?"

Did he know he had just coldbloodedly outlined his reasons for asking her to marry him? A chill shivered over her. "Then I guess we'll have nothing at all."

"You can say that after what we've just shared?"

She made no response, her throat far too tight and too strained for her to utter a word.

The bitter, dry voice went on, "This is to be the sum total of our relationship, then, one night together?"

"I suppose . . . it is."

"May I ask why?"

"A marriage should be based on . . . on more than physical need." This was dangerous territory, a mine field, and she didn't want to tread in it.

"What . . . more?"

The dry, cynical words made her bristle. What right did he have to make her feel she had hurt him? She stepped directly into the fire. "Love," she said bluntly.

Silence echoed in the room. Then he said softly, "You don't love me?"

Stung, she cried, "Yes, of course, I do, but you . . ."

". . . haven't said the words, have I?"

"No," she said, "you haven't."

"Once before I told a woman I loved her. It meant nothing."

She'd known. Deep inside her, at some primitive level, she'd known. It didn't make the hurt any easier to bear.

He said, "Suppose I never say the words. Suppose I live with you, cherish you, take care of you, stay with you day after day until the day I die, but never say the words. Does that mean I don't love you?"

"If your thoughts are with someone else . . ."

"I've thought of nothing but you since that first night you kissed me." He gripped her tighter in his arms. "Nothing. Even while I was hating my wife for wanting another man, I wanted you. And I'll go on wanting you. I'll never have enough of you."

He buried his face in the long strands of hair that lay fanned out on the pillow beside him. "I've asked you to spend your life with me. I can't do any more than that to show how deeply I feel about you."

He raised his head and looked at her. "Will you marry me, Raine?"

Her resistance fled. She told him yes with her voice and her lips and her hands and her body.

They were married a week later in the church in Verylon. When it was over, Julia hugged her close and whispered in her ear. "He's given you a marvelous gift, you know. He's given you his trust. He must love you very much, Raine."

When the reception was over, and Julia had taken a sleepy Tate home after assuring Jade that he would be fine with her for a week, they got into the car to drive to the Black Hills where they were going to spend their honeymoon. Then she thought about Julia's words. *He must love you very much.* Could it be true?

Jade said, "You're very quiet." He reached out and pulled her across the seat, his warm hand hard on hers. She went willingly. All he had to do was touch her and she melted. "Did I tell you how very beautiful you looked this afternoon coming down the aisle to me?"

She shook her head, her throat suddenly full. "I don't think you mentioned it." How light and casual her voice sounded.

She wore a knee-length apricot silk dress that had a full skirt and a sleeveless bodice over which she wore the matching cropped, waist-length jacket. She had found the dress on a flying shopping trip to Sioux Falls. She had especially liked the tapered sash that went round her waist and tied to one side. The tail ends of the sash lay on Jade's trousered knee. He held the wheel with one hand and casually fingered the silken tie with the other. "I like your dress very much," he said softly.

"Thank you."

"I think I'd like it even better if, tonight, for me, you wore just the sash."

It was the kind of bold, provocative statement Jade loved to make. He'd said similar things often in the week before they were married, and his words never failed to bring the bloom of color to her cheeks. They hadn't had time for this stage of intimacy before but Jade was making up for it with a vengeance. He hadn't made love to her physically the week before their marriage, but he'd made love to her verbally in a way that made her heart pound and her head reel. The sweet, provocative words took their toll. With each passing day, she had fallen more deeply under his spell.

And so, after they arrived at the hotel in Sioux Falls and ate dinner, she went into the bathroom to change and came out wearing nothing but the silken sash tied in front with the ends dangling in just the right place.

Jade had already showered and was lying in bed, waiting for her.

She came toward him, her smile the only evidence of her nervous courage. "Is this what you had in mind?"

He looked up and his dark eyes burned over her. "No," he breathed in a deep smoky tone. "*You* are what I had in mind."

She woke in the night with a throat that felt on fire. She groped around in the dark and found the modest robe she'd included in her packing. She went to the bathroom and got a drink of water, but it tasted of sulphur and did nothing to quench her thirst. Leaving the bathroom door open a tiny crack so that she could see, she found her purse. There was a soft drink machine in the lobby and she was dressed decently enough even if there was a stray desk clerk around.

She made it down the stairs without seeing anyone other than the sleepy young man in uniform who sat at the desk. He looked up briefly but when he saw where she was headed, his gaze flickered away.

She had just put money in the machine and heard the clunk of a can slipping into the tray when a fire bell began to ring. The sound was ear-splitting. Was it a real warning of fire? She smelled no smoke. Surely it must be a false alarm. Whatever it was, she had to get back to Jade.

She turned to race up the stairs. Instantly, the desk clerk materialized at her side and grabbed her arm. "Where are you going?"

"I have to go back up. My husband . . ."

"Sorry," he said unsympathetically. "You've got to go

outside. Your husband will come down without your help."

"No," she said, panicking. "I want to go to him . . ."

He caught her arm. "You can't go up there. You'll be in the way of those who are coming down. I must insist that you go outside."

In despair, Raine looked up the stairway. A mother was shepherding her three small children down, urging them on in an agitated tone of voice every step of the way. She knew the young man was right. She couldn't risk the possibility of harming a child. Jade would come down with the others.

Raine went out into the chilly night air and turned back so she could see who came out the door. But when pajama-and-robe clad people stopped pouring out of the motel, Jade was not among them.

"Is it a false alarm?" a worried female voice asked.

"We think so, but we can't be sure. Is everyone out?" the harried young man asked the group.

An older man, balding and with a paunch that prevented his robe from closing over his pajamas in front, shook his head. "There's some guy up there looking for his wife."

"Didn't you tell him to come down?"

"Hey." The older man shrugged. "That guy is twenty years younger, six inches taller, and in a hell-of-a-lot better shape than I am. I wasn't going to tell him a thing."

"It's Jade," she cried and before anyone could stop her, she raced past the crowd back into the building.

She pounded up the stairs two at a time and jerked at the fire door. It was heavy but she got it open. She screamed his name.

"Raine!" He had evidently been opening doors, going through the rooms one by one. Now he strode to her, his hair disheveled, his dark brown robe barely covering his hard thighs. "My God! I thought . . ." He gathered her into his arms, almost crushing her in his fierce embrace.

In a voice strangely thick and muffled, he said, "I thought I'd lost you."

"I went downstairs to get a soft drink." She pushed away from him to look up into his face. "Why didn't you come down?"

"I wasn't leaving until I found you."

She knew then that in those dark, husky words, Jade had declared his love for her as surely as if he had carved it in stone.

She went up on tiptoe to kiss him. She was a whisper away from his mouth when he said in a rough tone that still contained a trace of his worry for her, "If the building's burning, don't you think we should . . . go outside?"

She contented herself with covering his face with kisses. She touched her mouth to his lean cheeks, his amber eyelashes, the hard bone of his jaw, the firmness of his throat. As far as she was concerned the whole building could collapse around her and she didn't care. Jade loved her. "They think it's a false alarm."

As if to confirm her words, the mother with her three children burst through the door. The woman stopped in mid-sentence, cast an embarrassed look over their embracing figures and said brightly, "It's a false alarm. The management says it's perfectly all right for us all to go back to bed." Her fractious children tugged at the skirt of her robe. "It's all right. Daddy's waiting for us in Rapid City and he won't want to see us all tired and bleary-eyed now, will he? Everybody jump in bed and to-morrow . . ."

The door closed behind her. "You heard her," Jade murmured. "She said we should all jump in bed." He turned Raine in his arms and guided her into their room.

Inside, he pulled her around to face him. "Don't you agree?"

She looped her arms around his neck. "I don't feel very tired."

"Then," he said, his voice silky, "we'll have to think of something else to do."

"I could go back down to the lobby and get my soft drink . . ."

"You're not going anywhere," he murmured, his hands going to the tie at her waist. "I'm not letting you out of my sight." With an easy expertise, he slid the tie loose and pushed the robe off her shoulders.

A month later, on a very hot day in May, the printer who had bought the Linotype machine came and took it away. Raine hadn't been there for the actual loading, but now she stood with Jade and looked around the empty print shop.

She asked, "Why did you buy this place?"

"I bought it to give you a choice. I wanted you to have another option besides me. But you didn't take it. Are you sorry?" he said softly.

She told him the truth . . . as she had learned to do. "No." It didn't seem a big enough word for the overwhelming sense of love she felt for him. He had been thinking of her, only of her, and she had misjudged him horribly.

He perched on the corner of the desk, a look in his green eyes that she had come to know. It was an arrogant male look combined with a possessive pride. It was the way he looked at Tate—and now it was the way he looked at her. It was his look of love. "I had the printer make a souvenir before he disconnected everything."

"You did?" Her curiosity was aroused. She wouldn't have thought Jade would understand how sentimental she was about that silly machine.

He levered himself away from the desk and went round to open a drawer and pull out a slug of type. His eyes dark, he handed it to her.

For a moment, the backward letters made no sense. When they did, tears sprang to her eyes. In her hand she held the mirror image of the words, *I love you.*

He shrugged but she knew him well enough by now to know that his apparent unconcern hid a deep vulnerability. "You can use it for a paperweight, or . . ." his tone held amusement, "as a weapon if a calf should ever come after me again."

She set the line of type down on the desk and threw herself into his arms. "I love you so much, Jade." Her voice trembled. "I'll always love you."

"I know," he breathed, "I know." The unsteadiness of his tone made a little spur of excitement shiver over her, and when he folded her in his arms and pressed his mouth against hers in a deeply satisfying kiss, she kissed him back with all the ardent passion she was no longer afraid to express.

YOU'LL BE SWEPT AWAY WITH SILHOUETTE DESIRE

$1.75 each

1 ☐ James
2 ☐ Monet
3 ☐ Clay
4 ☐ Carey

5 ☐ Baker
6 ☐ Mallory
7 ☐ St. Claire

8 ☐ Dee
9 ☐ Simms
10 ☐ Smith

$1.95 each

11 ☐ James
12 ☐ Palmer
13 ☐ Wallace
14 ☐ Valley
15 ☐ Vernon
16 ☐ Major
17 ☐ Simms
18 ☐ Ross
19 ☐ James
20 ☐ Allison
21 ☐ Baker
22 ☐ Durant
23 ☐ Sunshine
24 ☐ Baxter
25 ☐ James
26 ☐ Palmer
27 ☐ Conrad
28 ☐ Lovan

29 ☐ Michelle
30 ☐ Lind
31 ☐ James
32 ☐ Clay
33 ☐ Powers
34 ☐ Milan
35 ☐ Major
36 ☐ Summers
37 ☐ James
38 ☐ Douglass
39 ☐ Monet
40 ☐ Mallory
41 ☐ St. Claire
42 ☐ Stewart
43 ☐ Simms
44 ☐ West
45 ☐ Clay
46 ☐ Chance

47 ☐ Michelle
48 ☐ Powers
49 ☐ James
50 ☐ Palmer
51 ☐ Lind
52 ☐ Morgan
53 ☐ Joyce
54 ☐ Fulford
55 ☐ James
56 ☐ Douglass
57 ☐ Michelle
58 ☐ Mallory
59 ☐ Powers
60 ☐ Dennis
61 ☐ Simms
62 ☐ Monet
63 ☐ Dee
64 ☐ Milan

65 ☐ Allison
66 ☐ Langtry
67 ☐ James
68 ☐ Browning
69 ☐ Carey
70 ☐ Victor
71 ☐ Joyce
72 ☐ Hart
73 ☐ St. Clair
74 ☐ Douglass
75 ☐ McKenna
76 ☐ Michelle
77 ☐ Lowell
78 ☐ Barber
79 ☐ Simms
80 ☐ Palmer
81 ☐ Kennedy
82 ☐ Clay

YOU'LL BE SWEPT AWAY WITH SILHOUETTE DESIRE

$1.95 each

83 ☐ Chance	96 ☐ Milan	109 ☐ Simms	122 ☐ Trent
84 ☐ Powers	97 ☐ James	110 ☐ Palmer	123 ☐ Paige
85 ☐ James	98 ☐ Joyce	111 ☐ Browning	124 ☐ St. George
86 ☐ Malek	99 ☐ Major	112 ☐ Nicole	125 ☐ Caimi
87 ☐ Michelle	100 ☐ Howard	113 ☐ Cresswell	126 ☐ Carey
88 ☐ Trevor	101 ☐ Morgan	114 ☐ Ross	127 ☐ James
89 ☐ Ross	102 ☐ Palmer	115 ☐ James	128 ☐ Michelle
90 ☐ Roszel	103 ☐ James	116 ☐ Joyce	129 ☐ Bishop
91 ☐ Browning	104 ☐ Chase	117 ☐ Powers	130 ☐ Blair
92 ☐ Carey	105 ☐ Blair	118 ☐ Milan	131 ☐ Larson
93 ☐ Berk	106 ☐ Michelle	119 ☐ John	132 ☐ McCoy
94 ☐ Robbins	107 ☐ Chance	120 ☐ Clay	
95 ☐ Summers	108 ☐ Gladstone	121 ☐ Browning	

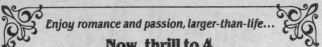

Silhouette Desire

Coming Next Month

Love And Old Lace by Nicole Monet

Burned once, Virginia had decided to swear off romance and settle for a sensible, chaste existence—but seductive Lucas Freeman stormed her defenses and neither her body nor her heart could resist.

Wilderness Passion by Lindsay McKenna

Libby wanted to be ready for anything when she met her unwilling partner on the environmental expedition. But nothing prepared her for Dan Wagner, and the mountain trek suddenly became a journey into a world of desire.

Table For Two by Josephine Charlton

Hadley and Lucas had shared a youthful love. Now, when Hadley had landed in his embrace once more, history repeated itself and left them both determined that this time they would not have to say goodbye.

The Fires Within by Aimee Martel

As a female firefighter, Isabel was determined to be "one of the boys"—but no one made her feel more a woman than Lt. Mark Grady. Passion blazed between them, but could they be lovers *and* co-workers?

Tide's End by Erin Ross

Chemical engineer on an offshore oil rig, Holly had vowed never to engage in a "platform romance." Kirk's touch could make her forget her promises, but would his dangerous job as a diver keep them apart?

Lady Be Bad by Elaine Raco Chase

Though Noah had broken her heart six years before, Marlayna still loved him. Now she would attend his wedding with only one aim in mind—she would break all the rules to have him back again.